CURSED PRINCESS CLUB
LambCat
I0823020

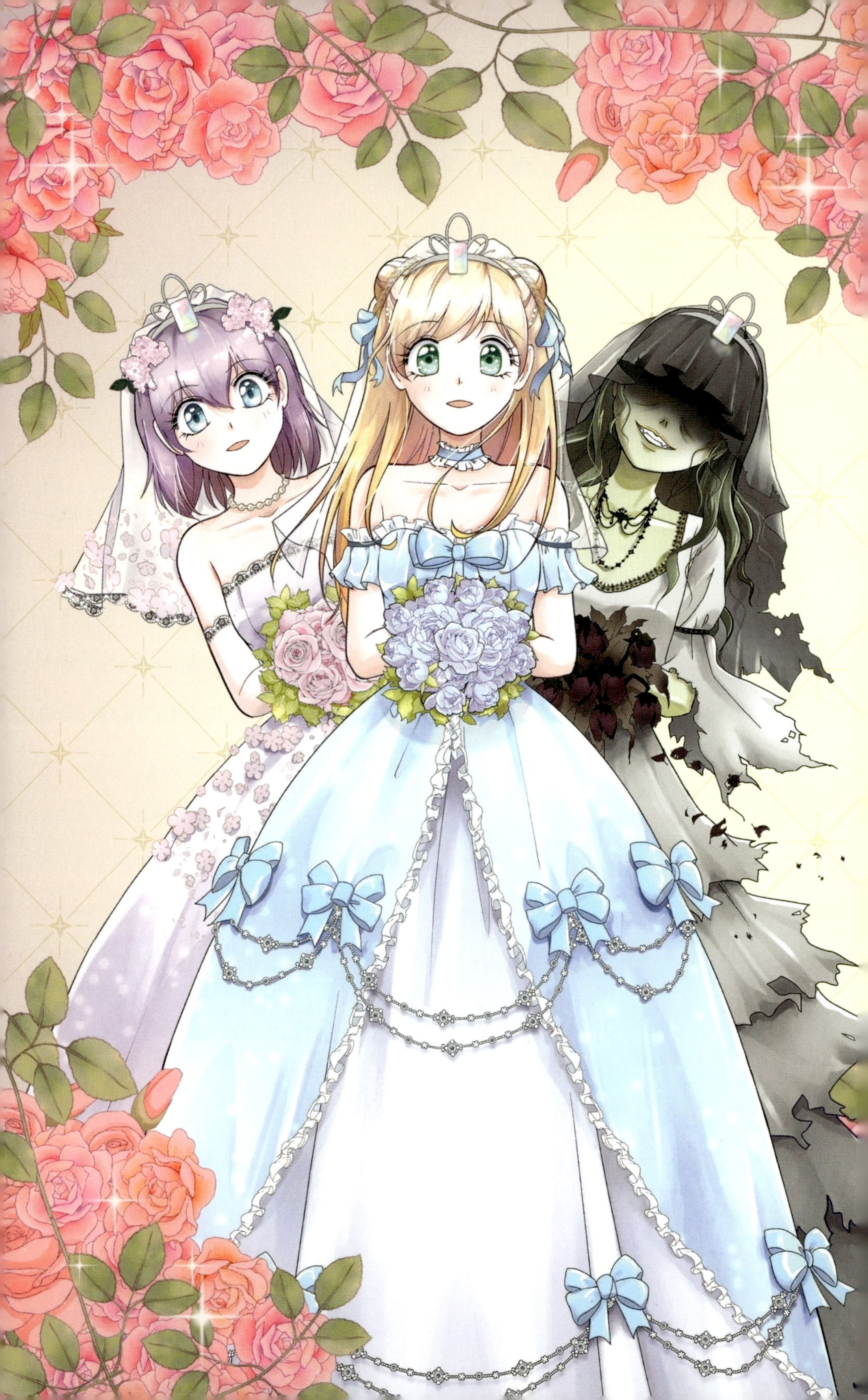

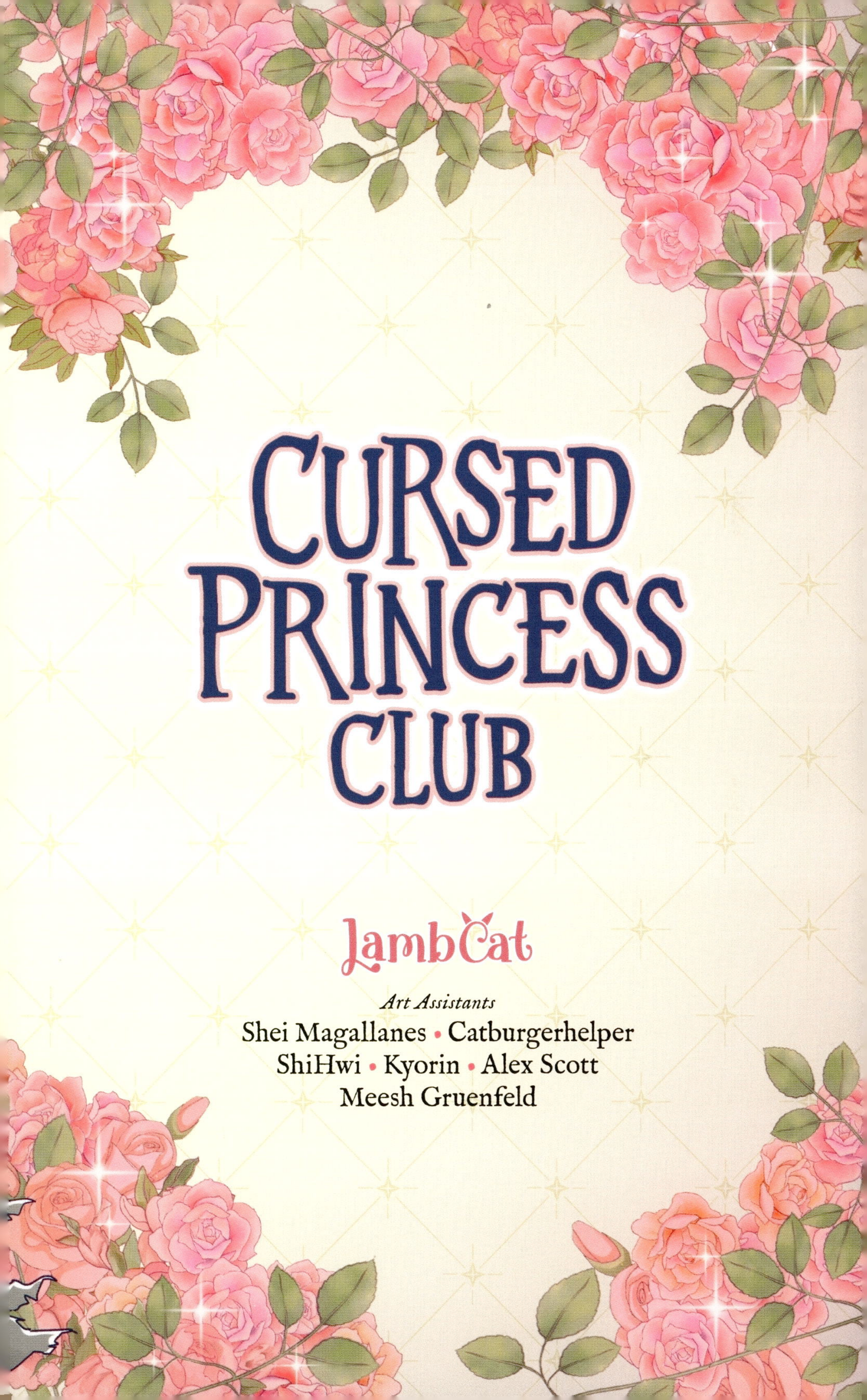

CURSED PRINCESS CLUB

LambCat

Art Assistants

Shei Magallanes • Catburgerhelper

ShiHwi • Kyorin • Alex Scott

Meesh Gruenfeld

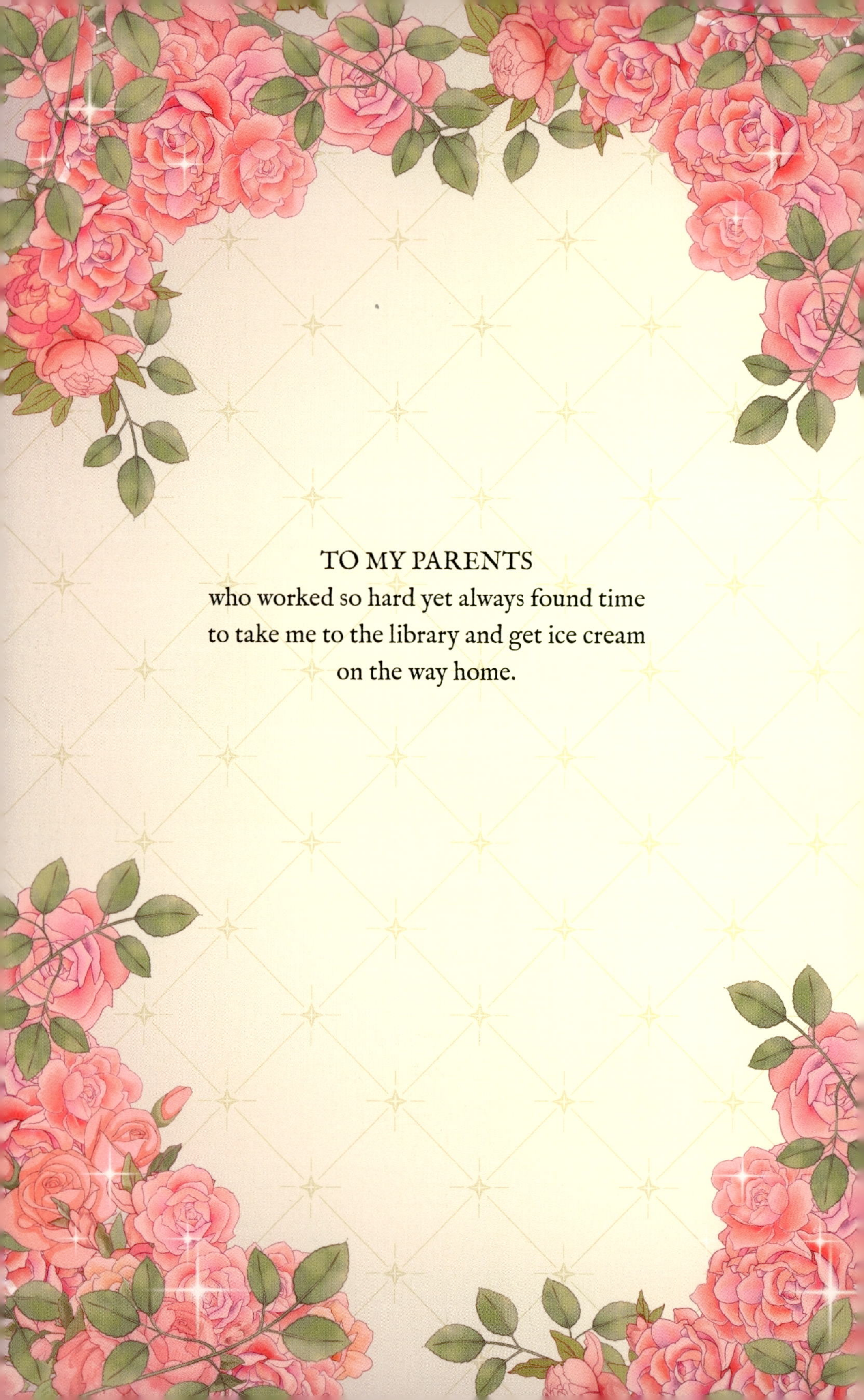

TO MY PARENTS
who worked so hard yet always found time
to take me to the library and get ice cream
on the way home.

Contents

BOBBIE CHASE *Executive Editor*
JOSH BEATMAN *Publication Design*
NIKO DALCIN *Sequential Story Design*
PATRICK McCORMICK *Production Manager*
EUNICE BAIK *Original WEBTOON Editor*

ARON LEVITZ *President*
ASHLEIGH GARDNER *SVP, Head of Global Publishing*
DEANNA McFADDEN *Executive Publishing Director, Wattpad WEBTOON Book Group*
DAVID MADDEN *Global Head of Entertainment*
TAYLOR GRANT *VP, Head of Global Animation*
LINDSEY RAMEY *VP, Head of Global Film*
SERA TABB *VP, Head of Global Television*
TINA McINTYRE *VP, Marketing*
CAITLIN O'HANLON *Head of Content & Creators*
DEXTER ONG *Managing Director, International*
RYAN PHILP *SVP, Operations*
MAXIMILIAN JO *General Counsel*
AUSTIN WONG *Head of Legal and Business Affairs*
COREY HOCK *Director, Legal & Business Affairs*
KEN KIM *WEBTOON CEO*

Published in Canada by WEBTOON Unscrolled, a division of Wattpad Corp.
36 Wellington Street E., Suite 200. Toronto, ON M5E 1C7
The digital version of Cursed Princess Club was originally published
on WEBTOONS.com in 2019.

www.wattpad.com

First WEBTOON Unscrolled edition: January 2023

ISBN: 978-1-99025-993-7 (Hardcover) ISBN 978-1-99025-979-1 (Paperback)

Library and Archives Canada Cataloging
in Publication information is available upon request.

Printed and bound in Canada

3 5 7 9 10 8 6 4 2

Prologue

CREAK
click
click
Heels?
Check.
Jewelry?
Check.
shine~
Dress?
Oh yes.
Ladies...

I think we're ready to have some fun tonight.

Shall we start with some champagne under the stars?
nod
Girls, wait.
rustle
rustle
Do you hear that in the distance?
DASH
pant
pant

rustle
rustle
I believe we have a new friend who's wandered into our forest...
Let's go say hello.
pant
pant
S-someone, please help!!!
No... *Stay away!!*
AAAAGGHHHHH—!!

Chapter 1

Much earlier that day in the small but vibrant Pastel Kingdom...
The king was returning from a lengthy expedition with his troops.

Hurrah!
Welcome back, Your Majesty!

Are you happy to be home, Your Majesty?
I will be, once I get to see each of my three precious daughters!

As soon as he arrived at his palace, the king rushed up the stairs.

He first went to greet his eldest daughter.
knock
knock
Maria, are you awake?
Come in!
CREAK
My beautiful Maria!
Princess Maria (age 18)
Father, you're home!!

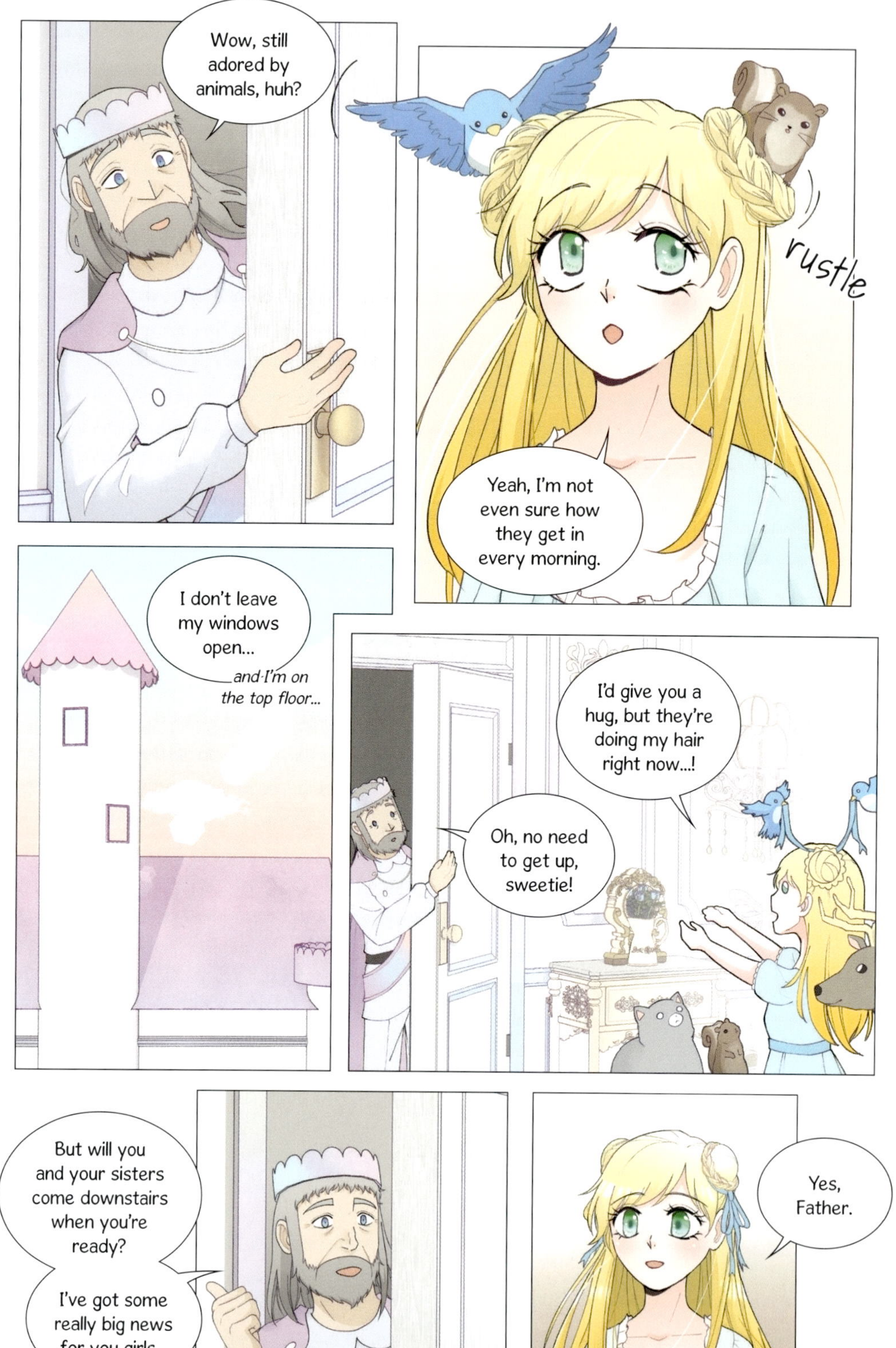
Wow, still adored by animals, huh?
rustle
Yeah, I'm not even sure how they get in every morning.
I don't leave my windows open...
...and I'm on the top floor...
I'd give you a hug, but they're doing my hair right now...!
Oh, no need to get up, sweetie!
But will you and your sisters come downstairs when you're ready?
I've got some really big news for you girls...
Yes, Father.

Next, the king walked to his second-eldest daughter's bedroom.
knock knock
Lorena?
Come on in!
Princess Lorena (age 17)
DADDY!

My vivacious child!
Those flowers still appearing out of nowhere, eh?
Yep, they just seem to grow wherever I sleep.
Can you come downstairs when you're ready?
Okay, I will.
He then went to visit his youngest daughter.
Are you up?
KNOCK KNOCK
My little Gwendolyn...!
FWOOSH
DAD!! YOU'RE BACK!!!

Oh, hey, Son.
Forgot this one's
your room.
Still sleeping in
the nude, huh?
Prince Jamie (age 16)

Anyhoo, hope you've been well, James. Let's play some chess soon.

Sounds great, Dad!!
step
step

The king then went to the actual room of his youngest daughter.
Gwendolyn, are you Awake?
knock
knock

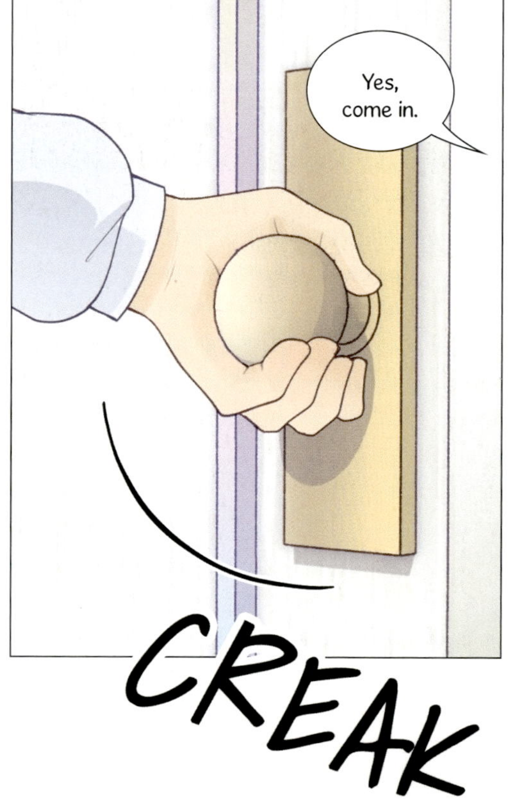
Yes, come in.
CREAK

Princess Gwendolyn (age 16)

Oooh, I missed my cutie pie!!!
I missed you too, Papa!!
I'd give you a hug, but—
Let me guess—that critter is doing your hair?
grrr
No, he's just... kinda stuck.
And as the king helped untangle his youngest daughter's hair, he felt a deep love for the simple pleasures of home.

At their father's request, the three daughters got dressed and gathered in the living room.

Hope we didn't keep you waiting, Father!
Not at all, girls. Have a seat.

ahem
As you girls know, we are not the richest kingdom...
and I often have to leave on long trips to assist our men.

I've made it hard on you, especially since your mother passed.
And for that, I am deeply sorry.

Yeah, you don't need to worry about us!
We're fine, Papa!

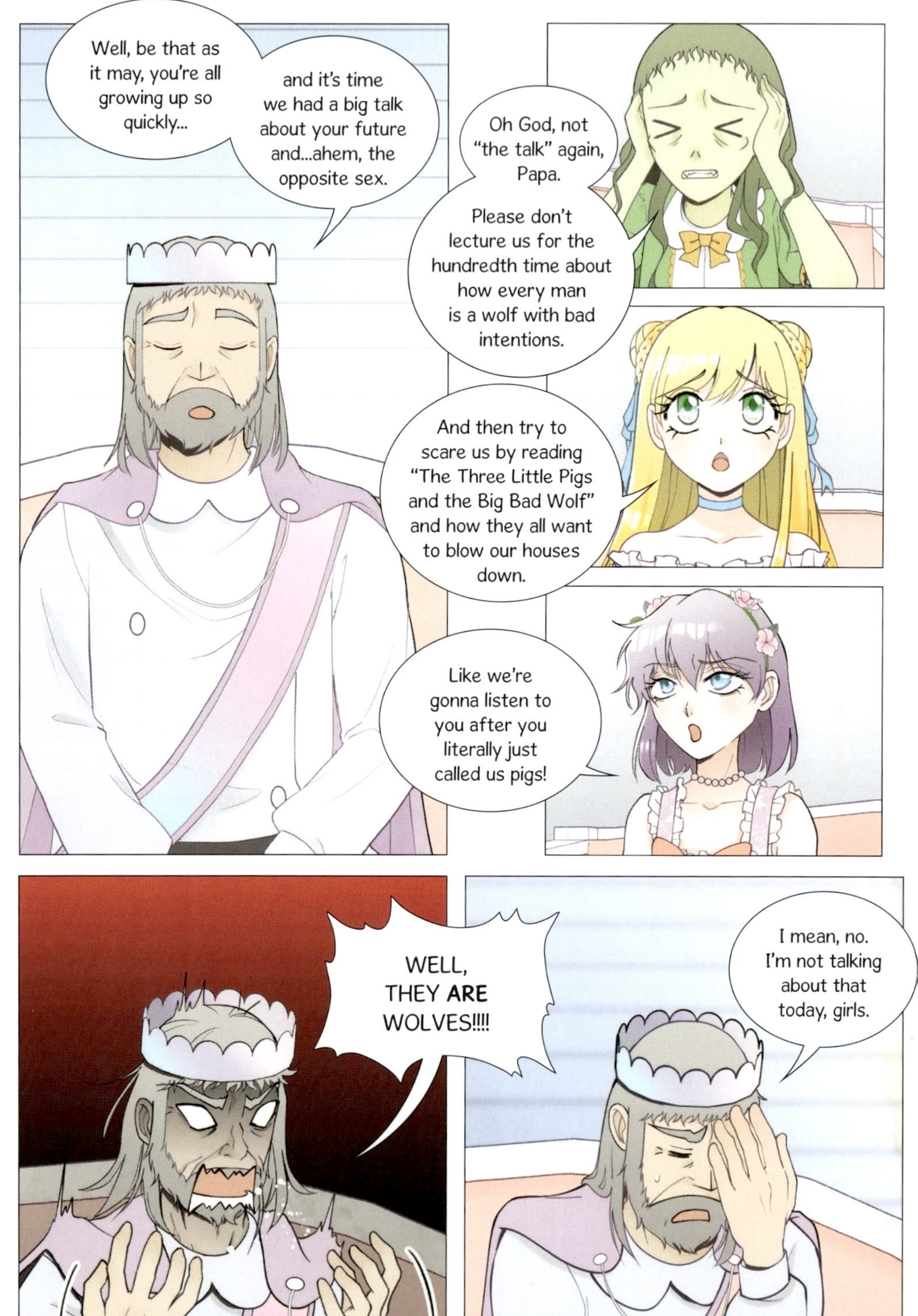
Well, be that as it may, you're all growing up so quickly...
and it's time we had a big talk about your future and...ahem, the opposite sex.
Oh God, not "the talk" again, Papa.
Please don't lecture us for the hundredth time about how every man is a wolf with bad intentions.
And then try to scare us by reading "The Three Little Pigs and the Big Bad Wolf" and how they all want to blow our houses down.
Like we're gonna listen to you after you literally just called us pigs!
WELL, THEY **ARE** WOLVES!!!!
I mean, no. I'm not talking about that today, girls.

I know.
I've had some strict policies about allowing boys into your life.
Yeah, you don't even let the male guards make eye contact with us.
But all of that changes today.
You know our longtime trusted ally, the Plaid Kingdom, right?
Plaid Kingdom
Pastel Kingdom
n
For many years now, we've been discussing the idea of unifying both kingdoms and strengthening our bonds.
Do you know what that means?
Yeah, it means an impending fashion disaster because pastels and plaid look gross together.
No.
It means I want to ask each of you to **marry** one of the princes from the Plaid Kingdom.
???!

Let me get this straight...

You never let us date, and now you're just asking us to marry strangers out of the blue?!

And it's only because it happens to be beneficial for both kingdoms?!

Well...

What do they look like?

Hubba-
hubba...
Oh
lordy...
Hhnnnggg...

THIS IS THE HAPPIEST DAY OF MY LIFE!
WE'RE GETTING MARRIED TO HUNKS!!!!!
BEST SOUVENIR EVER, DADDY!!
The three daughters frolicked at the great news their father gave them that day. 
They seem to be taking the news well.
My little pigs...!!

Sigh
Another boring day in the Pastel Kingdom...
I'm sleepy...Tell me something exciting you did last night, mate.

Hey! Being a guard for the Pastel Kingdom is not boring. It's a true honor!!
...And also no, I didn't do anything yesterday. I went to bed at eight.

tsk...
Why do I even bother?

...Hey, mate...

Ya ever wonder about this ol' haunted forest behind the palace?

No, because I have to face this forest every other day, and I like to not be terrified of my job.

Ignoring him
I heard rumors that once a month, in the middle of the night, a terrifying howl erupts from deep within the forest.
Howls like no human or animal could ever make.

SCREAM!

That...that came from inside the palace...! What's going on in there?!

Hunky prince husbands for everyone!!!
SQUEAL~!
Girls, calm down!! There are still plenty of details to discuss!
Oh, that's right.

What are their names?

Their ages?

Are they a big spoon or little spoon?

Let's see... that's Lance on the left (age nineteen)...

...Blaine in the middle (age twenty), and Frederick on the right (age seventeen).

And I suppose I can inquire about their silverware habits... *though I don't know why that matters...*

Since we're so close to the Plaid Kingdom, how come we've never heard of the princes?

That's because they've been in military academies since they were tots and went straight into serving their country.

I heard that the boys' perseverance was a real mental stronghold for their army.

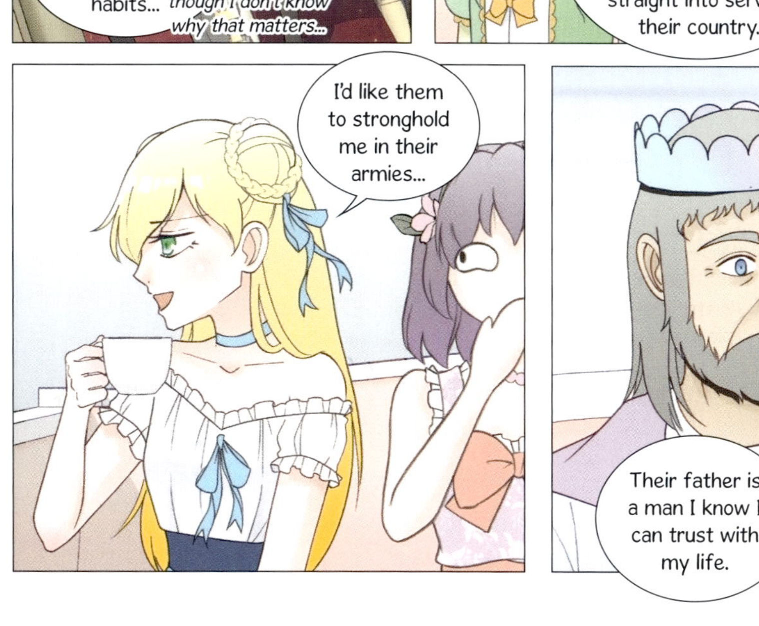

Do the princes know what we look like?

Yes. I sent them a portrait of all of you as well, and they wrote back saying,
"Each daughter's beauty is nothing short of Elysian."

"A **lesion**"?!
Hmm, they're not very good at compliments. But whatevs, they're hot.

So when do we get to meet them??

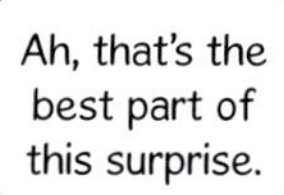
Ah, that's the best part of this surprise.
They're coming for tea today! At two o'clock!

tick
tick

Ahhblrglg...!
THEY'RE COMING HERE IN **TWO AND A HALF HOURS?!**

Now, my precious daughters, I want you to understand that your happiness and safety...
...are a million times more important than our relationship with the Plaid Kingdom.
But you may be wondering, "What exactly **is** happiness?"

Let me repeat a short tale from my past in which I found myself at the junction between the wildest joys and the most perilous dangers...
tip toe

I can't wear this to meet my future husband!
This is a **day princess** look for errands, like feeding swans or singing ballads from the balcony.
I have to break out my evening gown!

My possum ate my evening gown...

That's okay! I'll bring over some of my smaller gowns. Everything always looks lovely on you!

Thanks, Lorena.

Back in the living room...

And after months of hardship, we finally encountered the omniscient clam, and it proclaimed that...

there are short naps and there are long naps. And true happiness lies somewhere in between.

...Girls?

They went upstairs.

Oh, James... When did you get here?
A few minutes ago. Wanna play chess?
Uh, sure.

Son, you're blinding me here.
I can't see the board...

Chapter 2

The princes of the Plaid Kingdom are coming soon for tea, so I thought I'd bake some pies for the occasion.

All that's left is to bake them for forty minutes until the crusts are golden brown!

I wonder how Maria and Lorena are preparing for the princes...?

In Maria's room...
It pains my heart deeply to say this, but...
Goodbye, my first love. I'll never forget how much you've touched my soul...

...my sweet, brilliant Schozart.
I have so many wonderful memories of nights spent alone with you, humming your songs while stroking your marble cheek.

But I have someone else now.
SMASH

...Though I guess the engagement isn't a sure thing.
The Plaid Princes have to like us in person too.

They could meet us and decide they don't want to marry us after all...
Well, as the eldest sister, I'll just have to make sure that doesn't happen!!

...I'll keep him here just in case things don't work out...
push

All right. I'd better call my sisters immediately for a—
dash

TACTICAL MEETING! **NOW!!!**
BAM!

pull
We've all arrived at the conclusion that we need to make a **great** impression on the princes.

That's why I, the military genius of the family, have devised a three-pronged offensive strategy that will ensure our conquest.
OPERATION HEART-STOPPER
Here's how it goes...
When the princes arrive, we'll enter from the balcony with the advantage of high ground...
PHASE #1:
and Maria will unleash long-range fire with some sexy stares.
Too sexy!
My eyes!!
PHASE #2:
Next, I'll confuse them with some psychological warfare.
Hmph, you're not **that** cute. I can barely see your abs through your shirt.
What?!
PHASE #3:
And lastly, Gwen will enter into close-range combat through a blitz attack...
Whee!
...and tackle them into submission.
They won't know what hit 'em, but they'll be head over heels in love with us.
?!
Great plan, right??
PHASE #3:

Umm, I think it's a great start! However...it could benefit from one key addition.
You see, according to all the latest fashion magazines, attracting a prince may be only temporary...
HAIR EXTENSIONS
ONLY 399!!
VANITY FAIREST of them all
...but a good **bustle** will make them stay forever!
FASHION TRENDS
PRINCES LIKE BIG BUSTLES AND THEY CANNOT LIE
This could be our coup de grâce!
Now, being the most fashion-forward sister, I already snuck out and bought the new **Cinderella's Secret** Fairy God Bustle™.
It's an architectural marvel that provides three levels of increased lift.
But you can pretty much stuff whatever you like up there.
No need to overthink it.
..A lamp shade?
...Colonel Snuggles?!

All right! Now let's give them a try!!

Maria! Lorena! **Wait!!**
I appreciate all the effort you guys are spending to make sure the princes like us, but...
I think we're fine as we are, without any special tactics or... butt architecture...

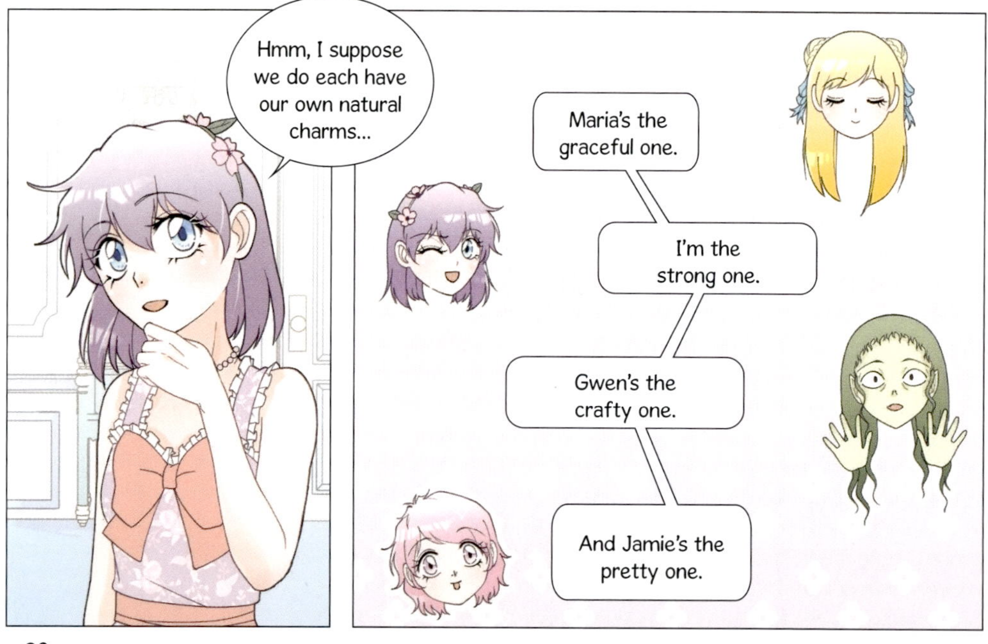
Hmm, I suppose we do each have our own natural charms...
Maria's the graceful one.
I'm the strong one.
Gwen's the crafty one.
And Jamie's the pretty one.

Can't argue with any of that...!
I guess I could forego the bustle and wear a simple-but-elegant dress instead.
Maybe I'll just go for a run to calm my nerves.
And I'm baking some p—
...pie...
Ack!! Sorry, Gwen!!
I FORGOT MY PIES IN THE OVEN!!!!
dash

Thank goodness I was able to take them out of the oven just in time!
Peach cobbler, apple, and strawberry rhubarb! That should be plenty!
I'd love to hear what the royal food critic thinks of them...
I think I have enough time!

clink
clink

Thanks for making time for me, Jamie!
No prob, Sis.

That's right. Jamie is the Pastel Kingdom's most influential food critic.

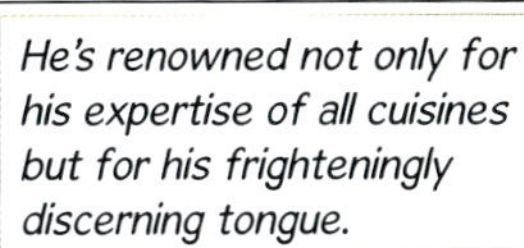
He's renowned not only for his expertise of all cuisines but for his frighteningly discerning tongue.

Chefs from faraway countries even visit to have Jamie consult them on their dishes.
Please tell me what you think of my *Escargots à la Bourguignonne*.
Hmm...

I detect refreshing hints of sage and brandy, but despite that...
it's overpowered by the sour taste of guilt from your affair with your sous-chef's wife.
WHAT?!
Uhhhh...

Jamie's critiques are always painfully accurate, and yet he's never said anything but sweet words about my cooking.

dash
INTRUDER ON THE PREMISES!
ALL GUARDS ON RED ALERT!!

Oh no!! Papa has been saying there's been an increase in crime and petty sorcery lately.
Jamie, we better get ins—

Why, hello! What a pretty princess you are...

Won't you have this delicious candied apple?

Um, excuse me...
Huh?!

May I ask what you're doing?

Oh!! Hey, my bad, sister!
You were clearly here first! I did **not** mean to encroach on your prey.

Us ladies gotta look out for each other, you know.

I'll just leave this here in case you need a little backup.

rustle
Toodles!

What the heck was that about?
Well anyways, let's—

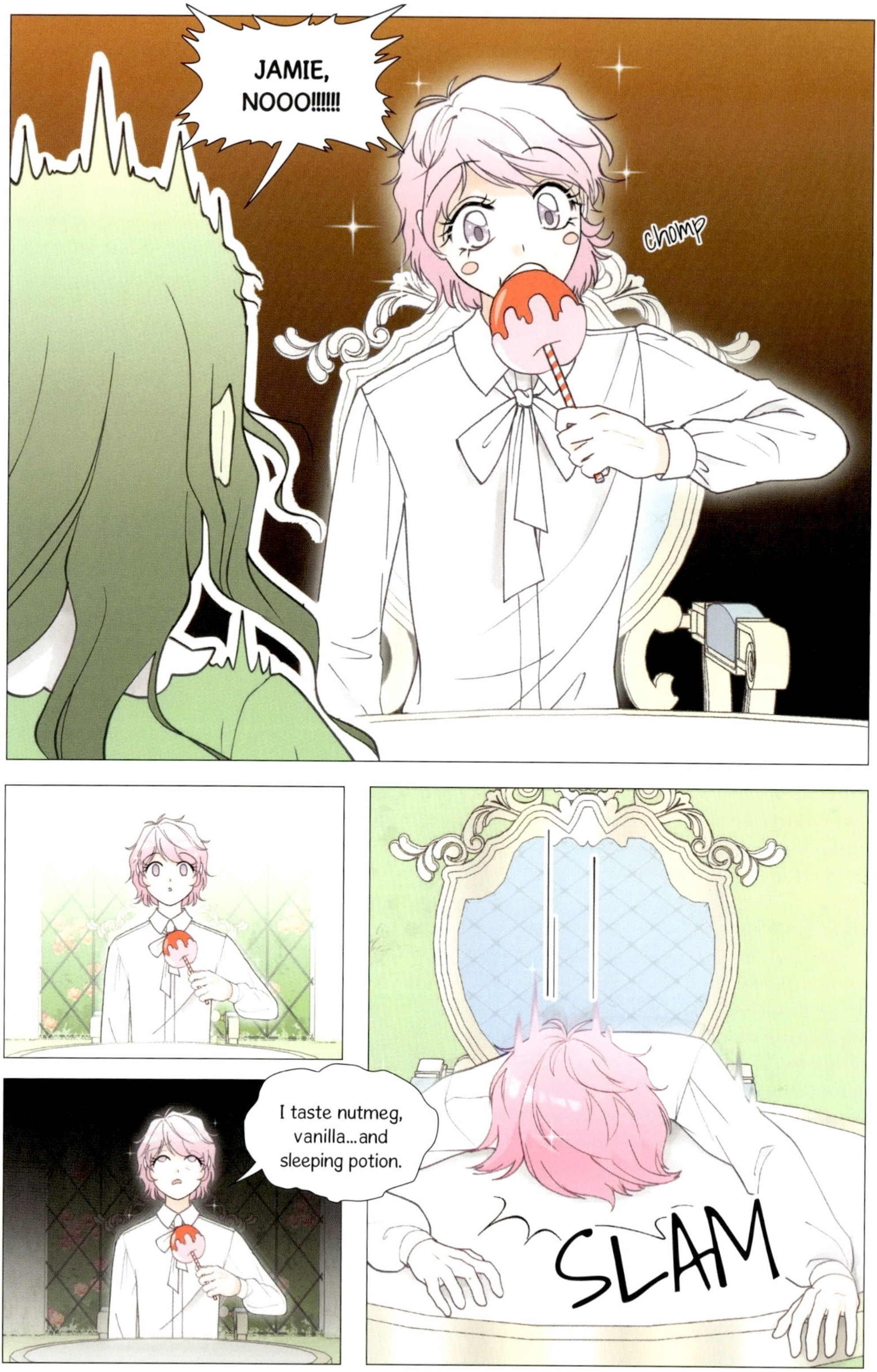

JAMIE, NOOO!!!!!!

chomp

I taste nutmeg, vanilla...and sleeping potion.

SLAM

Meanwhile, outside the Pastel Palace's front entrance...
step
heavy breathing
OMG the princes are here...

Holy crap, the princes are walking up the stairs as we speak!
And of course my bangs choose to be weird **now**!

I wonder where Gwendolyn is? I can't imagine her being late. Especially for our first chance to ever talk to boys.
Can't say we didn't try looking for her!

But even if she's late, the worst thing that'll happen is she gets the third-hottest guy on the continent.
'Cause it's first come, first served today.

I'm sure she'll pop her cute little head in at the last second.
So let's all go gather in the parlor for our guests.

step step
Pardon the intrusion, Your Majesty, but...

...the princes of the Plaid Kingdom have arrived.

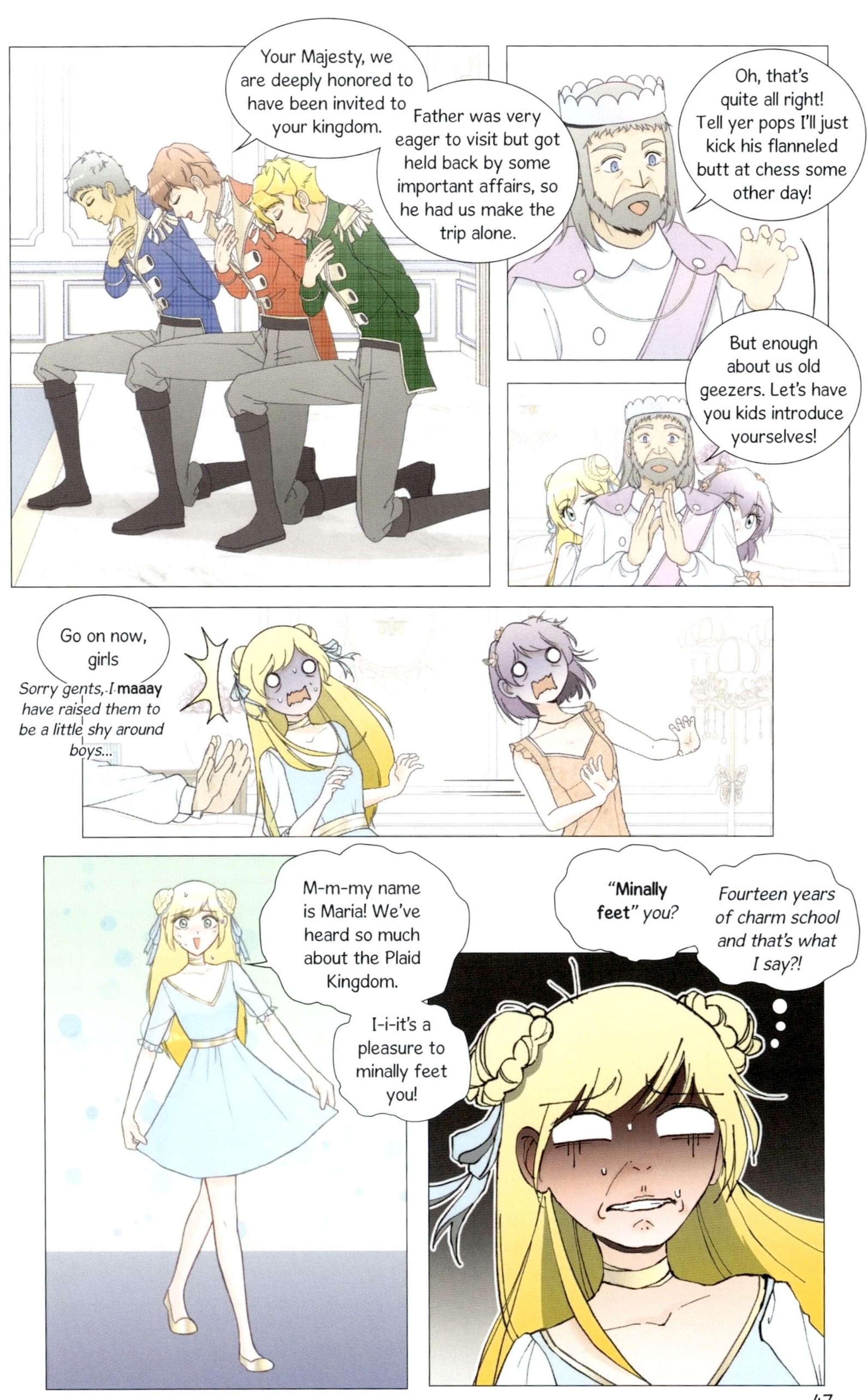
Your Majesty, we are deeply honored to have been invited to your kingdom.
Father was very eager to visit but got held back by some important affairs, so he had us make the trip alone.
Oh, that's quite all right! Tell yer pops I'll just kick his flanneled butt at chess some other day!
But enough about us old geezers. Let's have you kids introduce yourselves!
Go on now, girls
Sorry gents, I **maaay** *have raised them to be a little shy around boys...*
M-m-my name is Maria! We've heard so much about the Plaid Kingdom.
I-i-it's a pleasure to minally feet you!
"**Minally feet**" *you?*
Fourteen years of charm school and that's what I say?!

My name is Blaine, and the pleasure is all mine to be able to stand in the presence of someone so radiant.

Uhhh, hi. My name is Lorena. I'm super stoked to meet you all.
I'm Lance, and I think you're more beautiful than a million red roses.

Uh, hi, everyone. My name is Frederick, and...I thought there was a third daughter...?

Ya snooze,
ya lose,
li'l bro.
Shove it,
Lance!!!

She was the
only one I
was remotely
interested in
anyway...

Uh yes, she
is running behind
but will be here
as quickly as—

SORRY I'M
LATE!!!
Well, speak of
the devil! There
she is!
swing

Whoa...

There
she is!!

The most beautiful woman I've ever seen in my life.

What on Earth happened?!
Poisoned apple from a witch.
I couldn't stop it in time.
Z Z Z

I swear, that child gets in more trouble than a cat wearing boots.
Molly, can you please take care of the necessary procedures?
Right away, Your Majesty.

Well anyhow, now that all the daughters are here, let's get on with the marriage talks, shall we?

What?! But she looked *unconscious!!*
nod
Surely we can postpone things until your daughter has recovered!

What are you talking about? That was my **son,** James.
My daughter Gwendolyn was the one carrying him.
That was your **son**?!
THAT WAS YOUR **DAUGHTER?!**

B-b-but...
That can't be...
Th-the portrait...
I mistook his son for the youngest daughter?!
I just thought the youngest daughter was an evil spirit haunting the portrait!!
It happens all the time with portraits in our palace!
So...I was attracted to...
...and I'm about to be engaged to—
Please excuse my tardiness!
My name is Gwendolyn, and I'm incredibly happy to make your acquaintance.
Also, I baked some pies!
So please have a seat...

The girls served themselves some pie, eager to sit down and continue chatting with the princes.

Mm, the peach cobbler is fantastic.
Thank you!!
clink
So tell me, what books or fairy tales do you like to read?
Oh, I don't read fairy tales. They're a bit too sappy and childish for my taste.
Right, like your books about dragons and secret treasure are so realistic...
That's not true! Ya ever read the Crimm Brothers' version of Cinderella? That's the real stuff right there!

The wicked stepsisters can't fit into the glass slipper so they grab a knife and cut off their—
EW—!!

But then pigeons peck out their—
STOP!!!!

Do not make me vomit in front of company today.
Sorry.

Hahaha!

He's so shy... I haven't gotten to talk to him much at all...

Well, it seems like everyone is hitting it off swimmingly.

Shall we move along with the marriage arrangements?
Maybe have some royal dates and movie nights?
Chaperoned, of course...

Absolute—
I'd love th—
Uhh, **actually**, I just remembered... We promised we'd check in with father before we agree to anything.
So...we should really be heading out about now...

...Oh. Of course...
We've kept you for far too long...

pssst...
Frederick... what are you saying?
Dude...why are you ruining this for us?
Will you please just go along with me?!

Well, I'm not going anywhere.
There's still some pie left, and it's stupid good.
Lance, no! Put that down!

om nom nom
OW!!
STOP IT! STOP GRABBING ANOTHER SLICE!!!
SLAP

I wonder if it was because I was late and ruined everything...

...or maybe he hates pie...
Hmm, no. No one hates pie.

Sigh
I suppose we are under obligation to depart now.
I'm afraid I don't know when we shall meet again, but we do hope—

Pardon the interruption...
Your Majesty, arrangements for Prince Jamie's wake tonight have been taken care of.
I just need your approval for these invitations before we send them out.

A **wake**?! My God! Your son **died**?!
That's awful...

No no, a **wake**. Y'know, short for "wake-up ceremony"!
It's a social event in our kingdom where people from all over gather to try to wake the sleeping beauty—er, person...

Oh. Uh...Yeah, that's not how that term is used generally...

You'll stay for it, right?
It's customary to attend a wake of someone you've met!
And Jamie was poisoned when he helped Gwen with these pies...
so we're all a little responsible...!
Pleeease?

Yeah, pleeease?
Agh, stop! You guys are creeping me out!

...We will attend. It's the only right thing to do.

The sisters were elated to spend more time with the princes and secretly thanked their brother for his misfortune.
We owe you one, Jamie boy.

Outside the Pastel Palace...
All right, gather 'round, everyone!
We've got a wake happening here tonight!

So we need to split up and deliver these invitations A-S-A—
SWOOP
WHY?!

Nice one, mate.
Oh, come on...!

Why, hello.
What do you have there?

Oh? It seems like there's a wake being held at the Pastel Palace tonight.
Shall we join in the festivities?
Haha, don't worry. I was just joking.

You are cordially invited to...
The Wake of Prince Jamie
Tonight at 6:00
Pastel Palace
Ballroom C
Games, prizes, clowns, and more!
i've fallen asleep and i can't get up plz halp
Z
Z
Our kind probably wouldn't be allowed up there.

Chapter
3

Welcome to the Wake of Prince Jamie

Don't forget to sign the guest book!
Thank you for attending on such short notice!

I can't believe it! We convinced the princes to stay for Jamie's wake...
but we've been swamped with royal duties and haven't gotten to spend any time with them!
Now, now, if I'm to allow you girls to start joining these mixed-company events...
then at the very least, you must first do your due diligence of greeting our gracious guests.

Wonderful evening for a wake, Your Majesty.
Hey, Carl, thanks a lot for comin'. How's the farm been?

Oh fine, just fine...
Great googly moogly, are these your daughters?!
You've been hiding them since they were toddlers, and I can see why! They're hotter than fudge on a sundae!!

I'M TORCHING YOUR CROPS BEFORE YOU MAKE IT HOME, CARL!!

I can't stand any more of this.
Go find the princes and don't leave their side.
Really?!

And tell them they have my permission to slay anyone who so much as looks at you!!
I can't wait to ditch these dorky tiaras!
dash

Hey, Gwendolyn... is anything wrong?

Oh, um... I've just been...
wondering if maybe Prince Frederick doesn't like me very much...

pause

Gwen, I don't think it's possible to dislike someone as beautiful inside and out as you.
Prince Frederick does seem a bit shy, though.
So give him some time, and I'm sure you two will hit it off.

And if anyone ever makes you feel less than awesome, well, we don't want anything to do with them.
Okay...thanks, Maria. Thanks, Lorena.

Frederick! I've had enough of your terrible attitude today.

Remember that everything we do is to aid our relationship with the Pastel Kingdom.

You can do it, Clarissa! Kiss the dreamy prince!

Become a Pastel Princess!

You lost the dare, after all!

Okay, you got this... It's just a kiss...!

thump

thump

Wow, he's...
he's...

TOO PRETTY!!!!!!

I CAN'T DO IT!!!!!

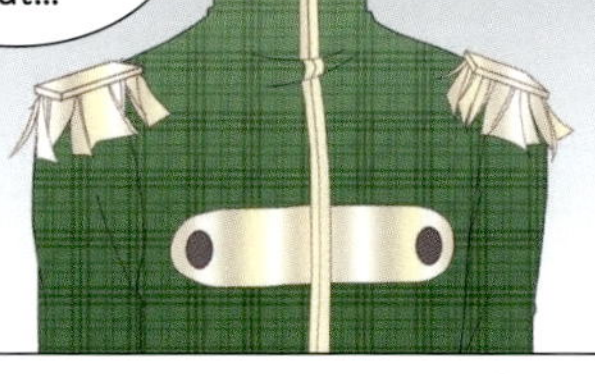
Well, that didn't work out...

Well, if none of these silly maidens can get the job done, I guess I'll just have to give it a try myself...
Me too!
Me next!
T-to save the kingdom...!
I don't think I like this tradition...

ahem
Ladies and gentlemen, I'd like to pause our festivities for a moment...
to thank you all for participating in the wake of Prince James.

We know that Prince James would have wanted everyone to enjoy his favorite meal with him.
Therefore, we'd like to announce that the waffle bar is now open for all guests!
Oh dear!
SPLAT
Oooooh, chocolate-strawberry swirl—!
Gasp The prince has awoken!
Your Highness!
...True love, indeed.
Jamie!!

chatter

chatter

Go ahead. Please don't worry about us.

We don't wish to impose on your limited time with your brother. We'll introduce ourselves after he's had time to recover.

But when you're done, I'll be waiting for you on the balcony to say good night.

Oh! I bet Jamie would appreciate a fresh waffle!

The one that woke him landed in his lap, after all.

I know Jamie's favorite toppings, so I'll go make him one and meet you guys at the infirmary!

WAFFLE BAR

Ohohoho... let's get you dressed up real nice...

Would you like to partake in a waffle, Frederick?

NO. What I would **like** is to go home!!

Okay, that's it.
grab

What's your problem today?!
My **problem**?!

My problem is that you and Lance got beautiful fiancés, and well, I got the short end of the stick!

What are you talking about?! We all saw their portrait beforehand, and you were the most excited!

Well yeah, I know! But... it was the portrait!
Remember? We **all** thought Prince Jamie was a princess!

Well, **I** most certainly did not.
WHY ARE YOU LYING?!
I KNOW you did when we looked at the portrait, and when we saw him in person!
You and Lance were entranced by him!

...Mm no, I have no clue what you're talking about.
@!#$%@#...
As the princes argued, they failed to notice a noise from the opposite side of the room.
rustle
rustle

step
step

Oh! Good evening, Your Highness! What brings you to our humble kitchen?
Hello, Chef Martina. I'm just passing through to the waffle bar.

I'm gonna make Jamie his all-time favorite waffle.

How nice, his favorite—

Wait. Good heavens, you don't mean **that thing**, do you...?!
My stomach hurts just thinking about it...
Er, I mean— Please don't allow him to eat that too often, okay?

We wish for our young prince to live a long and vigorous life!
Okay, I won't. I promise!

Compose yourself, Frederick!
Compose this, you jerk!!!

All right, time to get to work!

First, take a waffle and slather it with a hefty amount of strawberries and whipped cream.
Add a second layer and repeat. Top with a third waffle.

Next, cut a hole all the way down the middle of the waffle...
...and fill the hole with a handful of random toppings and sprinkles.

Lastly, drizzle the waffle with butterscotch sauce and place a ring of marshmallow bunnies on top.
Jamie calls it "Magical Friendship Volcano Surprise."

Just one last bunny to make it complete—

slip
Whoops!

Oh no, I need that!!
Wow they're really bouncy...
whee~

It looks like it went under the table.

this food sucks -goldilocks
Marshmallow bunny, where'd you go?

Ugh, what's with all these sweets? I'm on a diet, and I can't eat **anything** here!
crawl

Well, young miss, it's not your wake.
Here are some fajitas. Why don't you eat those?
No!! I'm on a no sugar, no fruit diet, you **idiot**. And fajitas have bell peppers!
Don't you even know that bell peppers are **fruits**?!

Please, bunny... where are you...?

Back at the other end of the waffle bar, Blaine and Frederick continued to argue.

So then is the issue that you'd prefer courting Prince Jamie?

Because we can see if that could be arranged.

What?! No, of course I don't want to date a prince, Blaine!!

Well then, Gwen is a lovely alternative.

No, she's not! She's NOT lovely, and you **know** that!!

For once, just get off your high horse and admit it!!

Frederick, lower your voice.

Ugly...
Gwendolyn is...
REALLY UGLY...

...!

...

Uh...what was I doing again...?
Oh, right... I'm here to make a waffle for Jamie...

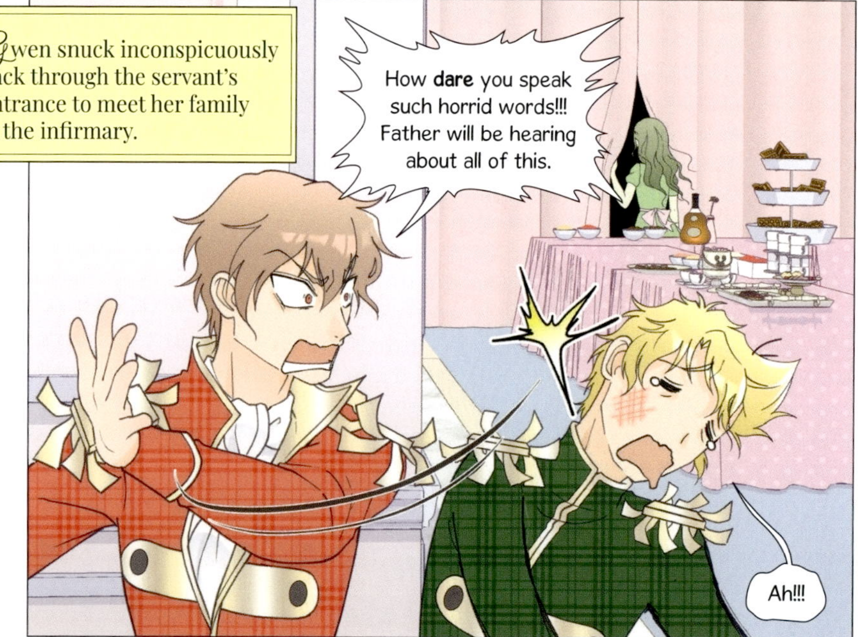
Gwen snuck inconspicuously back through the servant's entrance to meet her family at the infirmary.
How **dare** you speak such horrid words!!! Father will be hearing about all of this.
Ah!!!

Pastel Palace Infirmary
Thanks for visiting me!
Congrats, you're awake!
Of course! Thank goodness you recovered completely!
I'm sad I didn't get to meet the princes, though. So what do you think of them?
I want to climb Blaine like Jack wants to climb a hunky beanstalk.
I've never wanted to be pie so badly in my life.
Huh?
Can we please not say these types of things when Papa's around?
Blaine can speak five languages! So hot!
Lance can eat eleven slices of pie! Unexpectedly hot!
Okay, Papa will just sit in the grave he dug and try not to die inside...

creak
Hello?
Gwennie!!!
Jamie, I'm so glad you're okay!!!
I brought you your favorite...
step
step
MAGICAL FRIENDSHIP VOLCANO SURPRISE!!!!
Um, so actually...
Congrats, you're awake!
...I was thinking of heading to bed now. I'm feeling pretty sleepy.
Of course, cutie-pie. It's been a really long day.
Just be sure to say a proper goodbye to the Plaid Princes, okay?

...Um...
Yes, Papa...

Good night, everyone!
Sweet dreams, Gwen!
Good night, sweetheart!

Mmm, I'm starving!!

아
Marshmallow bunny...why do you taste like carpet?

step
step

All I have to do is turn right down the hallway, and I'll eventually run into the princes.

step
step

dash

What...
...am I doing...?

Where...

...am I going?
All I know is...
...I just want to get away...
I always thought that all princesses, by nature, are beautiful.
I guess not.
I always assumed that all princesses would meet their Prince Charming and fall in love instantly.
Nope.
I always thought bell peppers were vegetables.
Don't you even know that bell peppers are **fruits**?!
I was pretty sure about that one too...

GASP

OH MY GOD!! SOMEONE, PLEASE HELP!!!!

NO!!! PLEASE, STAY AWAY!!!!

THUNK

BAM!
AAAAHHHH!!

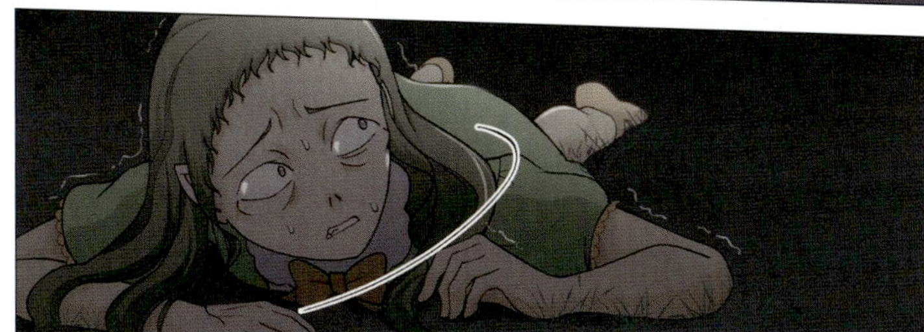

No...I'm going to die here, away from my family...
I'm thankful for every day I got to spend with them...
step
step

But they have the princes now...

...and I was just going to get in the way...

Chapter 4

...And where am I??

chit
chat

step
step

Oh...!
She's up...

She's awake...
The girl is awake...

Why are people staring at me and whispering?

Gwendolyn is...is... REALLY UGLY!!!

Right...
I guess the truth is... I'm ugly...

...and these girls seem to all be beautiful, glamorous princesses of some kind.

They're probably whispering about how I look...

tap
Uh, hey there, kiddo.

Sorry about last night...
Huh? Wh-what do you mean?

Well, it seems like you ran into our forest, had a bit of a tumble, and fainted.
But I think we may have accidentally given you a scare.

oops...
You never know who's wandering around these parts.
But once we saw that you were no threat, we brought you here and patched you up.

Oh, that's right...
I ran out of the palace yesterday without thinking.
I sprinted all the way to the haunted forest?!
And the terrifying figures chasing me were actually these women?
Thank you for treating my wounds and letting me stay the night.
Please let me know how I can ever repay you.
Well aren't you the most polite little vagabond we've ever met!

Vagabond?! No, I'm a princess!! Just like you guys!
Though I may not look it, apparently...
Princess...? Just like us...?

Oh! Of course!! How could we not notice?

Hey, everyone, she's one of us!!
You don't have to worry! Come and say hello!
?

Oh, thank goodness!
That's wonderful news!

It's so nice to meet you! Have a seat!
Whoa!

And please have some wine!
Um... No thanks, I'm sixteen.
Also the clock back there said it was seven a.m.

POOF!
Hi!! I'm **sooo** relieved!!

Did that crow just turn into a girl?!

No, no, no, do not serve the poor girl this wine!!!
tsk
tsk

Honestly, you ought to know!!!

Wow, she looks so elegant...

When it comes to wine, **redder is better**!
L-Lobster claws...?! *Why does she have those?!*
What the heck is this place?!
tap
Hello, pardon me!

I'm Princess Jolie of the Lace Kingdom. I hope you don't mind, I changed you into one of my nightgowns after you fell last night.

Oh, thank you so much! That was very kind of you.
Of course. We're so happy to have another friend in our club who understands us for who we truly are.

What is this "club" exactly...? And what does this girl have in common with the others...?
Oh, I think you have a piece of lint in your eye...

Oh, really?

lift
Thank you for letting me know!

* screaming internally *

Before we start, I suppose I should introduce myself.

My name is Princess Calpernia of the Polygon Kingdom.

I'm the founder and president of this club.

We all call her "Prez," though...

And I'd also like to introduce our guest—
Er, sorry, kiddo...What's your name?

Oh, I'm Princess Gwendolyn of the Pastel Kingdom!
But um...can you tell me more about what the Cursed Princess Club is?

Sure, I can give you the official spiel.

So, Gwendolyn, you're familiar with fairy tales, right?
Yes, my family loves them!
nod

Well then as you know, in your typical fairy tale, princesses often face difficult perils...
Must touch pointy thing...
...and become cursed with an awful affliction.
The curse is always broken just in time...
...for her to have a happily-ever-after with Prince Charming.
But, well, in real life... it's not always that simple.

You never read about the princesses whose curses don't get mended completely...
or about when there are no known remedies for their curse.
I'm sorry, but it's the best we can do.
I think you look...festive...

And ladies? What unattainably high expectations does society have for princesses?
That we always look young and beautiful!
That we live perfect, inspirational lives!
That we have fingers!!

So we, the cursed princesses, are hidden or even locked up by our families, unfit to represent our kingdoms.

I'm just gonna go pick up some, uh... porridge...
Be right back, babe!!
And the notion of a Prince Charming or a happily-ever-after quickly fades away forever.

Therefore, I decided to take one of my family's old vacation homes...
that happened to be located in your quaint kingdom...
and turn it into a secret sanctuary that cursed princesses can escape to.

I want this to be a place where we can support one another...
...and remind ourselves that we are still beautiful and worthy of happiness, no matter what any person or prince thinks!

Yet it's mostly just a place where we eat junk food and hide from the world.
moved to tears
Yes, there's still much room for improvement...

Anyway, welcome to the Cursed Princess Club Headquarters!

Umm, why does the front of this mansion look so much more run down than the back?
Oh my, is it that noticeable?
The carpenters I hired to fix up the place left halfway through for some reason.
And I can't seem to get anyone else to come out.
Several months ago...
tap
tap
tap
Where are the carpenters? I've got an urge to make some eyes-screeeam...!
lift
Is that so? I feel like **slicing** them up...
...some fresh fruit—
Where are they going...?
?
aaaaaaahhh

All right! Next, let's go around and introduce ourselves and our curses.
sip

Who wants to go first?

How about you, Monika?
pfffft
Who me?! B-b-but...

Umm... Well okay...
My name is Princess Monika of the Quilt Kingdom.

When I was little, I was taken hostage by an evil wizard...
gasp!

...and turned into his pet crow.
POOF!

He was eventually defeated, and I was turned human again.
But for some reason, I still transform into a crow when I get... um...um...
Crap, I hate talking in front of people...

Um...when I get...
...ANXIOUS...
POOF!

slurp~
Excellent! Who's next?

I guess I'll go next. I've gotta go soon and start my homework anyway.
Oh, she looks like she might be my age!

Hey. I'm Princess Abbi of the Neon Kingdom. I'm fifteen.
I guess she's younger than me...

I was given a box that would supposedly bring me everlasting happiness as long as I didn't open it.
Sooo yeah, I opened it.
And now I look like an old lady, and the doctors say there's no cure. It sucks.
Bobby was about to ask me out too, but now he's just, like...really respectful to me.
How... awful...?
Okay! Let's have you go next, Saffron.
Sounds good.
I'm Saffron from the Foliage Kingdom.
Wow, these princesses all embrace their diverse looks wholeheartedly and confidently!!
I'm so moved!!
I'm not a princess!!! I'M A **MAN**!!!
I recognize that look of admiration in your eyes!!!
O-oh, sorry...

Ah, right. I should mention that we have some male members.
But the name *Cursed Princess Club* was already well established, so we just never changed it.

CURSED PRINCESS CLUB
It's mostly because I already had a lot of T-shirts printed with that name.

I **hate** it! You need to change it ASAP!!
Oh, hurry up and state what your curse is.
Ugh, okay...

My curse is that I can't grow out a full, majestic beard like all the other men in my royal lineage.

stubble
It's a horrible, despicable curse.

That's **not** what your curse is.
Ughh **fiiiine**, you party poopers.

twitch
I guess I also have this evil hand that a goblin cursed me with.
I can't control its movements, and it terrorizes people around me. But it's really not that bad.

So what's your curse, Gwendolyn??
Uh, what? I don't—

Ooh, let us guess!!

Oh, I got this! Did you switch bodies with a witch?
No! I...
Is that what I look like...?

I know. Were you an old mop that got brought to life?
I got a buddy who used to be barbecue tongs...
What?! **No!!!** I...

Were you—?
I don't have a curse, okay?! This is just how I've always looked...
I didn't mean to join the Cursed Princess Club.
I just accidentally stumbled here from our palace after a bad night. I'm sorry.

whoops...
POOF!

How do you guys keep thinking that game is a good idea...?
But I guess I'm the one who first assumed she had a curse, so it's really my fault.
Prez, do something, please...!!!

Okay... Hey look! It's eight o'clock, which means it's time for morning affirmations!
Gwendolyn, please join us. They're really uplifting!
It's eight o'clock already?!

I have to get home before my family wakes up and finds out I was out all night!

Well hey, kiddo. Why don't you come back sometime?
I can't help but think there's something on your mind that our little club can maybe help with.
Despite the idiotic things we do sometimes...
Yeah, please come back!! We'll make it up to you!
We didn't even finish introductions!

Really? Even though I don't have a curse?

Ummm... yeah, I'd say you're good...!

It's practically one.

A minor technicality, really...

I think I'll pass...

Gwen ran briskly out of the forest back toward the Pastel Palace.
I hope everyone's still asleep at home!
All right, guys, time for affirmations. Repeat after me!
Curse or no curse, I am a pretty princess who deserves love.
Again, I'm **not** a princess...
Don't ruin the vibe, Saffron.

Chapter 5

step
step
Maria, Lorena, and James all seem well rested from yesterday's myriad of festivities.
I must say— from meeting the princes to the wake, everything went splendidly!

It's time to say good morning to my favorite cutie-pie!
knock
knock
Gwen, are you awake?
Hellooo, Gwen??

She must still be sound asleep...!
CREAK
Rise and shine, my little—

Gwennie pie...?

WHO TOOK MY BABY GIRL?!

GUARDS!! MY BABY'S BEEN KIDNAPPED!!!
DEPLOY ALL TROOPS AND ARTILLERY IMMEDIATELY!!!
step
step

P-Papa!!
Oh! Gwen!
Uh...stand down, guards. My bad...

Where were you, sweetie??
I...I woke up really early this morning, so I went out and gathered some wildflowers from the garden...
I can't believe I'm lying to Papa! I'm sorry!!

Ooh, my little early bird! It's just like you to do something adorable like that!
You had me worried, though!
That's also such an adorable new nightgown!

Wait a second...!!

He knows I'm lying!!

Is that a **bandage**?! Did you hurt your arm?!

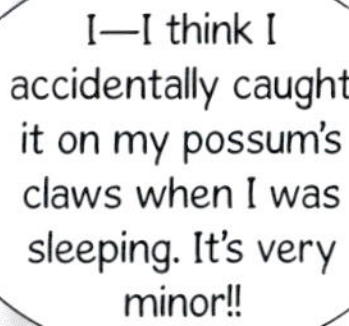
Papa would be furious if he knew I ran into the haunted forest...!
I—I think I accidentally caught it on my possum's claws when I was sleeping. It's very minor!!

IF THIS LEAVES A SCAR, I'LL PERSONALLY RIP OUT EVERY NAIL AND TOOTH FROM YOUR VILE BODY!!!
What did we do?!
I'm sorry, Mr. Possum!! I'll bring you extra treats for a month!!!

Morning, Gwen!!! How'd ya sleep last night??
step
step

I'll go put these pretty flowers in some water and leave you to your girl talk...

Um, I slept pretty well!
So what did I miss between you two and the Plaid Princes last night??

Nothing big... I just talked with Blaine about music on the balcony for a while...

Who's my favorite composer? I love Schozart!
I love singing along to his operas though, like "The Magic Sousaphone!"
Er, I mean, not as an imaginary lover or anything, haha...That would be weird...

I adore "The Magic Sousaphone!" Please let me hear you sing it!
I'll learn the music and accompany you on piano! Although I'm not the best at it...

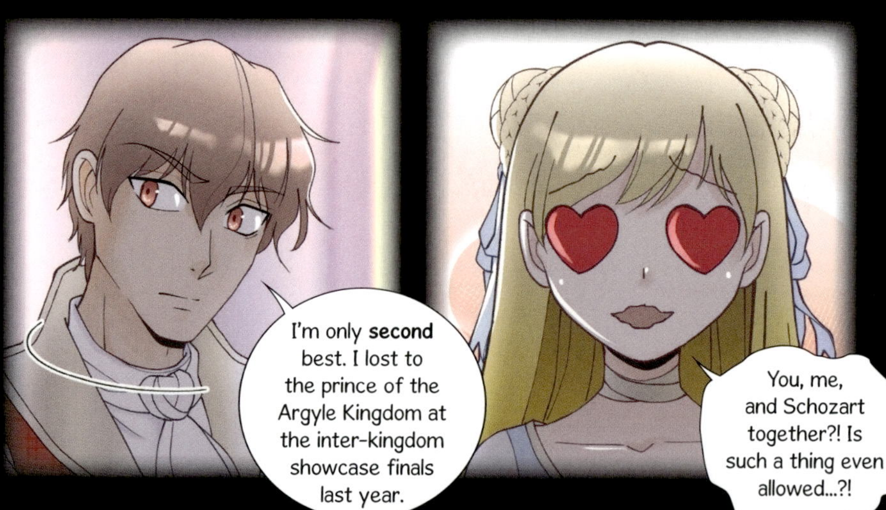
I'm only **second** best. I lost to the prince of the Argyle Kingdom at the inter-kingdom showcase finals last year.
You, me, and Schozart together?! Is such a thing even allowed...?!

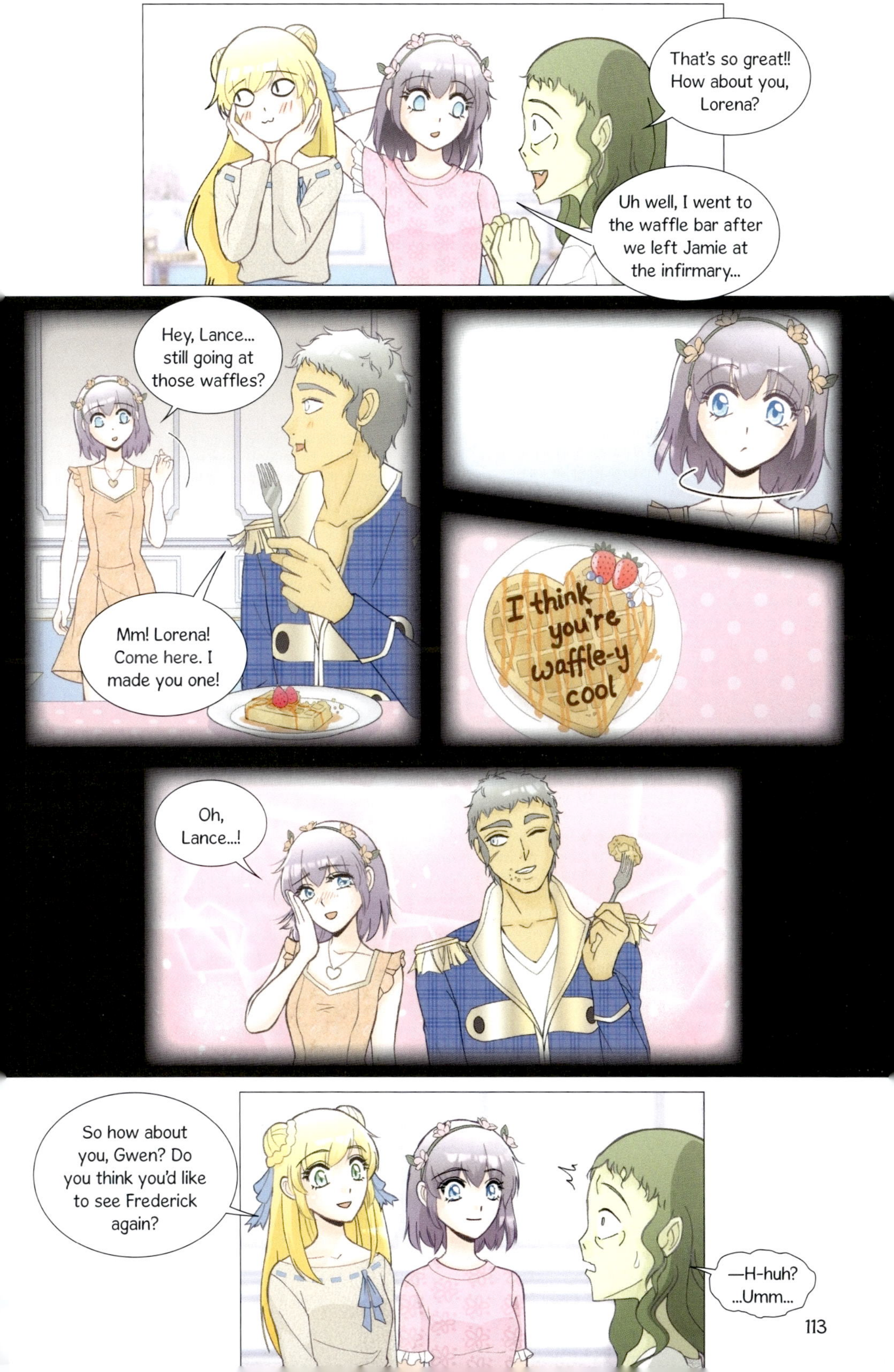

Hey, Lance... still going at those waffles?

Mm! Lorena! Come here. I made you one!

I think you're waffle-y cool

Oh, Lance...!

Yes...!
Of course...
Uh, were you guys headed down for breakfast? I'll get changed and meet you there!
Oh! Okay, we'll see you downstairs, then!
step
step
What do you think's for breakfast?
I think it's waffles for the rest of the month...

Maria and Lorena would defend me at all costs, even if that meant cutting things off with the Plaid Princes entirely.
And that would break my heart. I've never seen my sisters so happy...
I don't know what I should do...

Well hey, kiddo. Why don't you come back sometime?
I can't help but think that there's something on your mind that our little club can maybe help with.

I don't think I'd ever be desperate enough to wander into that place again...
tug
tug

Figure it out later! You promised us treats!!
tug
I guess I can figure it out later...
Why is your dad so scary??
tug

That same morning in the not-too-distant Plaid Kingdom...

knock
knock
knock

Ugghh... Yes, come in.
Ow, why does my face hurt...?

Morning, li'l bro. Dad wanted me to come get you for breakfast and to tell you that...

...he's royally pissed.

sip
clink

Okay...don't panic. Lance said Father's angry, but... he might not be angry at **me**.
He's pretty much **always** angry...!
pull

G-good morning, Father...
step
step
Ah, good morning, boys...

Ah—not so fast, Lance. You know the rules.
Last person seated at the table has to do 30 push-ups.

What?!
But that's because when I came here earlier, you told me to go upstairs and get Frederick!

My sons, I uphold these rules because they train you for the harsh realities of life...

harsh realities that even your old man can fall prey to.

For instance, take your visit to the Pastel Kingdom yesterday.

I couldn't wait to visit. I wanted to embrace my dearest old friend, the Pastel King, who I miss very much.

I wanted to be there as our children fell in love, as we set wedding dates in place, and as our kingdoms grew closer.

But last minute duties popped up, and as the ruler of our glorious land...

So imagine my surprise when I sat down to breakfast this morning to ask my eldest and most-preferred son how their excursion went...
and he told me all about how...

...YOU SCREWED EVERYTHING UP, FREDERICK!!!!

...you wasted months of planning, and now the Pastel King thinks I'm **hesitant** about uniting our kingdoms!!!
I let my guard down, and YOU—my stupid, selfish worm of a son—made a **fool** out of ME!!
CRACK
What do you have to say for yourself, Frederick?!

Oh God. I have to do this. I have to stand up to Father, just this once!!

Be strong!!! Your happiness depends on it!!
Umm, w-with all due respect, Father...

...I REFUSE TO MARRY GWENDOLYN!!!

I **do** care about strengthening our alliance with the Pastel Kingdom!
But Blaine and Lance are happy to go through with their engagements, which means the kingdoms will be successfully merged!
So it frankly **doesn't matter** if I marry Gwendolyn or not!!!

Whew... I said it. I really said it...!
Now just stand your ground and act calm. Father will have no choice but to back down...

Whooosh
thunk

Did you say it "doesn't matter" if you don't marry Gwendolyn...?
Do you have **anything** inside that permanently cowlicked, vomit-colored head of yours?!
Anyone who knows ANYTHING about the pure and unbreakable bond of sisterhood...
can foresee that if even one of those sisters is rejected by our family, **all** the other sisters will reject their marriage engagements out of solidarity.

Why does Dad know so much about the unbreakable bond of sisterhood...?
So if you can't understand that your lack of affection toward one sister DOES affect all sisters...
DOES affect our entire alliance with the Pastel Kingdom...
and therefore, DOES affect our kingdom's prosperity...
...then you'll be trading places with that bagel.

So, Frederick...
you're all going back to the Pastel Kingdom again this weekend.
And this time, you're going to show Princess Gwendolyn just how devoted you are.
And I'm canceling all my plans to come along and make sure of it.

Butler, send a message to the Pastel Kingdom urgently requesting their hospitality again this weekend.
And make arrangements for three people to ride in the family carriage.
Three? Aren't you going to ride with us, Father?

Oh, I am. But YOU aren't, Frederick.
In order to teach you a thing or two about how to properly treat a lady...
you're going to take Laverne there.
pffffff
Did he say...?
I can't even...
I'm taking Laverne to the Pastel Kingdom?!
Meet Laverne, the Plaid Kingdom's most pampered llama.

Chapter 6

This
is simply
unacceptable!!!
CLASS IN
SESSION.
Do not interrupt!
What has gotten
into you children
lately?!
thwack
Now listen.
I know you all had
a very exhilarating
weekend.

But royalty is
about more than
just fancy parties
and handsome
suitors!
It is my duty
to ensure that you also
develop strong, creative,
and disciplined minds that
can guide and inspire the
people around you.
Today you
were each
supposed to hand in
essays about what
your extracurricular
study will be for
the year.
But **none** of you
wrote anything!!
I've never been so
disappointed in you
before!!

Miss Agatha,
I didn't do my
homework because
I was poisoned.

Sigh
Yes, I know, Jamie. You are obviously excused.
I meant it more for the ladies in the room, who really need to pull themselves together!!

Miss Agatha, why do I feel funny lately?
Miss Agatha, what is love??

Well, I...don't have the experience to educate you on such matters...
I mean, never mind that!
Since no one did their homework, let's have everyone state their extracurricular study plans in person right now!

Yes, Miss Agatha.

Shoot!!
I've been worrying so much about our engagement to the Plaid Princes that I haven't thought about school at all!!

Jamie, your career as a food critic has been prospering splendidly.
I take it you'll continue to expand your clientele this year?
Yes, ma'am!

And, Maria, will you continue your vocal-performance studies this year?
Yes, I would like to hold a recital next spring.

Now, Lorena... Last year, you surprised us with your one-woman rendition of Sun Wu's "The Beauty of War."
It was... intense...
What, pray tell, will you grace us with this year?

Glad you asked! I was thinking of keeping the focus on defense this year.
And I've got big plans, so I'll just tell you everything, starting from the top—

That's all right, Lorena. I'll just wait for your essay.
And make it one page or less.
Roger that, Miss Agatha.

And lastly, we have Gwendolyn.
What will your extracurricular focus be, dear?

I-I've never forgotten to do my homework before!!!
What's wrong with me??

Why does it feel like I've been messing everything up lately...?

Um... Miss Agatha, I'm sorry, but I—

CRASH!!
AAAAH!!!

AAAAAH!!!

AAAAAH!!! Oh my gosh, this poor little crow!!

...wait a second...
psst... Monika, is that you?
nod
Why did you crash through the window?! Is it...
that you still need your glasses when you're a bird?
nod
nod

gasp!
What is this? A letter??

"With great joy, we formally invite Princess Gwendolyn of the Pastel Kingdom...
to become a member of the... CPC"...?

My God, Gwendolyn...

That's the invitation to join the Cursed Princess Club?!
What do we do?! We're in so much trouble!!!!!

You **brilliant** girl!! You were accepted into **the** CPC?! The Cosmopolitan Princess Conservatory?!
That's the utmost renowned institution, exclusively open to only the most refined and elite princesses!!
Wha...?

This is the most ambitious extra-curricular study I've ever heard of!
I didn't even know they had a branch near our neck of the woods! They're very hush-hush, after all.
But they must have acknowledged your formidable baking skills and numerous other talents!!

Now see, children? **This** is how you think about your future!
Everyone, be more like Gwendolyn!!
Gwennie, you're amazing!!
Duh, Gwen's the best!

So I'll just confirm that you'll be attending their initiation ceremony this Friday at twilight...
Will you join the
Yes
No
...and we'll send this back to their admissions office posthaste.

SHOVE

toss
There we go. Now students...

...let's piggyback off of this inspiring news and have you write your essays now.
After all, nothing strengthens one's intentions better than putting pen to paper.
Yes, Miss Agatha.

scribble
scribble
Ahhh, sweet silence...

I suppose I was too harsh on them earlier.
They are good children, after all...

WHAM!
HEY KIDS! Guess what?!
I just heard from the Plaid King!
He and the boys are all coming to visit us again this weekend!! How exciting is that?!
SHRIEK~~~!!

Yaaay, I get to meet the Plaid Princes!
sob~
Our prayers have been answered...!!
Who cares about studying at a time like this, am I right?!
Let's get ice cream!
Yaaay!!
I wish I could do something about their father, though...!!

Later that day...
"If you accept this invitation, meet us at our secret location this Friday at twilight."
I guess that's tonight.
And I guess I'm attending, thanks to Miss Agatha...

I couldn't correct her and tell her I didn't get into some super-elite princess conservatory... Club.
Because if I did, I'd have to expose the truth about the Cursed Princess Club.

What have I gotten myself into...?

step
step
Hey, no cheating, Lorena! It's my turn to roll the dice!

I'm sorry that I'm missing game night to attend the Cur— **uh**, CPC initiation tonight.
THIRSTY THIRSTY PRINCESS
Here are some cookies fresh from the oven!

Oh Gwen, you shouldn't have!! We're so excited for you to enter such an elite conservatory!
Do you need a carriage drawn up or anything?
Yes, I rolled a six! I get a necklace and a date with Prince Justin!
Um... no, that's okay. There are arrangements for me...behind the castle...
Oh, what am I saying?! Of course a refined place like that would prepare your means of transportation!
I'm not hip to all these fancy schools, but I support this Cosmopolitan Princess Conservatory, if they recognize the brilliance of our little Gwen!
But I mainly support it because it doesn't sound coed.
I'm not a princess!!! I'M A **MAN**!!!
Well, I'm gonna get going now!
I love you! Don't wait up!
Have a great time, sweetie! I love you!
It's your turn now, Father.
Okay..."Your Prince Charming has been stolen away from you. Give all your jewelry to the player on your right."
What? **again**?!
I'm choosing the board game next time.

creak
Maria always says this is the best door for sneaking in and out of the palace.

shhh...
You see any hotties this weekend, mate?
I went to the dentist. My mom thinks he's fairly handsome.
WTF, mate...

step
step

step
step

rustle

...?
Hello, Gwendolyn.
Welcome to your initiation into the Cursed Princess Club.

We're really glad you decided to join the club! I honestly didn't think you would!
I didn't think I would either...

But before we can officially declare you a member, we have some... **prerequisites** for you to complete.

...Like what?
First, we ask you to vow to obey the five sacred commandments of the Cursed Princess Club.
And to help you remember these commandments, we have a little keepsake for you.
Jolie, if you would...
rustle

Our commandments follow a simple acronym: P.A.N.D.A.
So when in doubt, just remember Princess Panda!

I'll clip this to your backpack for you.
Panda...?

P
A
N
D
A
The P stands for...
"Prince Charming is not necessary for a happily-ever-after!"
Build your own happiness, Sis.

P
A
N
D
A
A is for "assist others"! We try our best to help each other and the community when we can!
A charitable princess is a sexy princess!

P
A
N
D
A
N means "Never tell anyone about the Cursed Princess Club." Ever.
For your own safety and the safety of the other princesses!

P
A
N
D
A
D stands for "Don't go near the barn."
Just don't, okay?

P
A
N
D
A
And finally, A stands for...
"Again. Don't go anywhere near the barn."

So what do you say? Do you vow to adhere to the club's rules?
Um... What's in the barn—?
Don't worry about it, kiddo.

Erm....I guess I wasn't planning on going into any barns anyhow...
Okay. I vow to obey the five commandments of the Cursed Princess Club.

Wonderful!!! Then we'll move on to the last little step—
The all-night trial!
The **what**?!

Yep, it's a test that some consider grueling, ear-shattering, extremely invasive, and mortifying.
But it's a wonderful tool for measuring one's character and perseverance.

And if your body remains after dawn, the other members will be the final judges as to whether you pass or not.

SLUMBER PARTY!!!!

Top 10 Fairy tale Hunks
BELLE MAGAZINE

Sooo...

How is this the grueling, mortifying, character-defining trial that Prez described earlier?
This is just a normal slumber party...
Wearing the nightgown she brought to return to Jolie

Well, those were actual complaints. Most were verbatim out of Saffron's mouth.
He just really hates slumber parties.

But slumber parties **are** truly a great test of one's character.
You can learn a lot about someone through all the laughter, stupid games, and lack of sleep.
Really?

Yeah! Take Prez and Saffron, for instance.
They gravitated right toward the ping-pong table, showing that they have strong athletic and competitive proclivities.
If I beat you, I get to be the new president of the Cursed Princess Club, and I'm changing the name!!

It's funny, you say the same thing every time, and yet you've never beaten me.
I take it as a sign that you're actually quite fond of the name!

ARRRGHHH!
The power dynamics between people quickly become clear.

Dang it, I just need one more bobby pin to finish Gwen's hair.
Jolie, you got a spare?
Yes, I do!

lift

Here you go, Abbi.
Thanks, boo.

What else is in there...?
Ooh, that's pretty and shiny! Can I have it??
No! This is for Gwen!

Aw yeah,
match point!!
You're **finished,**
Prez!!

twitch

What?!
Why does this
curse always
act up at the
worst times?!
No!!
Let go—
GRAB

thwack

Oh God,
what have
I done...

plop

Slumber parties are also a great way to observe how people deal with problems and confrontation.
Well, Saffron, as the continuing president of this club, my advice is this:
He who hits it, gets it.
pat
What a selfless leader you are.

But yeah... here I go...
Um...I'm really sorry, Jolie. I think we dropped something in your... skull...
That's okay, Saffron!
Thanks, you're always so sweet—
But you'll have to get it out yourself.

...k, no prob
Wow, you're right, Monika. This **is** very informative.
I hate slumber parties...
tee hee

I'm also realizing that I still don't know much about everyone here and their curses—
Ooh, learn about me next, then!

Remember me from your last visit? My name's Princess Syrah of the Metallic Kingdom!
Would you like some champagne?
Um no, no champagne. I'm still sixteen.
But yes, I remember you! Though I feel like you look a little... different...

Oh yeah, haha. **This,** right?
I must have had a good day when we met!
A few years ago, a jealous boyfriend suspected me of cheating on him.
So he gave me chocolates infused with the typical "Pinocchio's nose" curse to find out if I was lying to him.

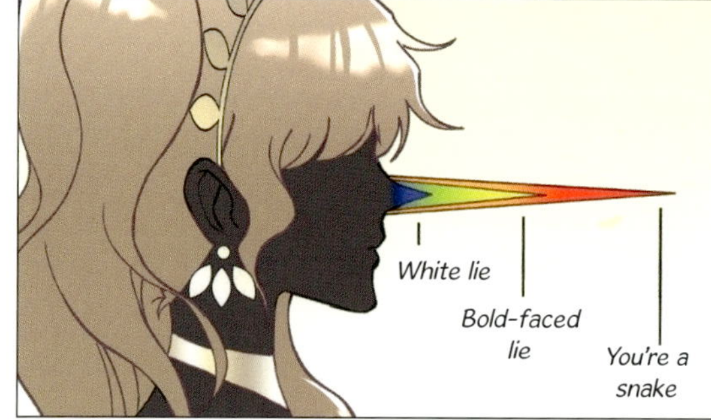
White lie
Bold-faced lie
You're a snake
And since then, every time I tell a lie, my nose grows in proportion to the severity of the untruthfulness.
But it always eventually returns to its normal size.

Wow. Did he feel terrible about what he did?

Um no, because he was right. I was totally cheating on him.
So I think he felt pretty good about the whole thing.
...oh.

But it's okay.
Unlike most of the other girls here, I don't let my curse hold me back from having a fun time with gentlemen suitors.
So if you ever need relationship advice or anything, I'm your girl!

Sooo, Gwen... do you have any gentlemen suitors or Prince Charmings in your life?

Oh! Um...Well, I guess...

Gasp
Really??
Wooow~!
Oooh, we wanna hear everything!!!

No, no!! He's just an arranged fiancé, and...I mean...
tug

He doesn't even...um...

Are these tears?
...Not now...!

Um, he doesn't even...

...want me...

G-Gwen...!

Hey, it's okay. Let it all out...
sob

Guys...please, help me...!! Something's biting my hand in here, and it won't let go!
Why isn't anyone listening to me?!

As the slumber party progressed, Gwen told the princesses all about her engagement to Prince Frederick and how she overheard his harsh words about her appearance.

All I can handle right now is how to face Frederick and move forward without ruining the engagement for my sisters.
You care about your sisters' happiness with the princes that much more than your own?
You'd understand if you saw the way they talk about them...
You're considerate, kiddo...way **too** considerate.
But I still think you should confront him about what he said and give him an earful about how a gentleman should properly speak about ladies.
It'll also give you some closure.
C-c-confront him?!
I can't do that!!!
Hmm...I agree with Prez. Talking to him is the right thing to do.
But it doesn't have to be confrontational, just honest.

Here, why don't I role-play what I would say to Frederick if I were you?
Abbi, you pretend to be Frederick, okay?
Uh, okay...
Hey, Gwen, what's this loser Frederick look like?

Um, he has big, pretty green eyes and blond hair that kinda goes... like this...
And then it goes like... that way...?
What...?

Okay, so I'm Gwen, and this is what I'd say once I ran into Frederick.

Hey, Frederick. Can we talk for a little bit?
Ugh, I'm busy doing my hair, which Gwen makes sound like a broom that dried at a weird angle.

But, whatever, talk if you want.
Sigh Okay, thanks.
You're making this really difficult...

I want you to know that I overheard what you said about me the other night.
It hurt my feelings, but I understand.
Busted...

I'm fine not being your fiancé, and I will stand on the sidelines as your friend and sister-in-law.
I just want you and everyone in our families to be happy.

Bruh...that's so big of you, especially when I've been such a butt.
He doesn't talk like that, you know...

So something like that! It takes the pressure off both of you to force a romantic relationship.
And he'll be stunned that you're so mature and confident.

That was really helpful advice!! I'll try to say that to him word-for-word!
Thank you, Syrah!!
My pleasure, babe...

And who knows! Prince Frederick could start to fall for Gwen the instant she walks away!
Boys are like that sometimes...
Right, Syrah?

Um... **Sure**!

grow

Hey! You don't think that at all! You were lying!
Well, you backed me into a corner!!! How's a girl supposed to respond to that??

You know there's only one way to find out what will happen in the future with men...

...You must consult the fortune-teller!!!
Ooooh nice, Thermidora!!
That's a staple of any successful slumber party!

Your name is Princess Thermidora?
Yes! Good evening, Gwendolyn. I hope you're enjoying your soiree.
I am, thank you!

Um, Thermidora? Would it be rude of me to ask what sort of curse turned you into part lobster?

Why yes, that **is** rude!!!!
I-I'm so sorry! I shouldn't have pried—

It's rude of you to assume I was cursed **into** a lobster, when it's quite the opposite!!
I am a luscious lobster princess who has been cursed into this hideous human body!!
A devious sea cucumber was jealous of my perfect relationship with Benedict, the most handsome Lobster baron.
She cast a spell to turn me human, so that I'd have to abandon my kingdom and the ocean altogether, choking for air.
Then she could keep my Benedict all to herself.
But thank goodness, she's an inept slug, and her spell left my immaculate pinchers intact...
gasp!
Eventually, Prez found me and kindly brought me to the Cursed Princess Club.
But still I sit in my room every night and sing about returning back to the sea in my true form...
Under the
I dunno, it's this weird song she sings all the time. Just let her finish...

Later that night...

It's fortune-telling time, everyone!!
crinkle
1
2

Saffron, you're going first. Pick a color.
What? No way. I'm not doing this junk.

Oh, you need to relax those shoulders and have some fun!
pat
pat

AAAH! Okay, okay! I pick purple!!

Wonderful! The fortune-teller predicts that...
...you will marry a whale prince, live in a toilet, and you'll give birth to 89 sea urchins.

Hahaha!!!
Well, I'm **pretty** sure I won't do any of that...

Your turn, Syrah.
Okay! I choose pink!

You're going to live in a mansion made entirely of egg salad, and no one will ever kiss you again.
Noooooo!!!!

Ooh, ooh, do Prez next!!
Sure, why not?
I pick blue.

All right! Let's see...
Prez is going to marry a poor man, live in a one-bedroom house with a white picket fence, and have four children.
Well that's not very funny. That's just...prudent and slightly endearing.

Hey! Doesn't that kinda sound like what you—?

Oh my God, I'm so sorry! I don't know what I was thinking...

I-it's okay, Monika.

rise
I was actually just gonna get up and refill some snacks...

What happened? Why does Prez look sad...?

...Come to think of it, what exactly **is** *Prez's curse...?*

Hey!!
What are you doing?!
Yank
I'm taking the fortune-teller away! It's making everyone feel awful!

SMACK!
OOF!!
Knock it off! I haven't told Gwen's fortune yet!!!

flop

PILLOW FIIIIGHT!!!

Aah!

Someone save me...!!

poof!
caw~!

Poor fool doesn't even see me coming...
EAT THIS!!!

Huh...?
catch

...?

Wait, did you **help** me for once, cursed hand?

My dude!!
Did you just high five yourself...?

rustle
laughter

fwoosh~
HEY!!

WHY ARE YOU ALL SCREAMING IN THE MIDDLE OF THE NIGHT?!

Oh! Hi, Nell. This is Gwen, she's the newest member of—

DO I LOOK LIKE I CARE?!
Just keep it down. It's late!!

She seems mad...!
Okay, we will! Good night!

...

...Is it just me or am I being glared at...?

That was Nell, the Striped Kingdom princess.
Don't mind her. She sort of does her own thing.
She is right, though—it's late and we should go to bed.

I am pretty beat...!

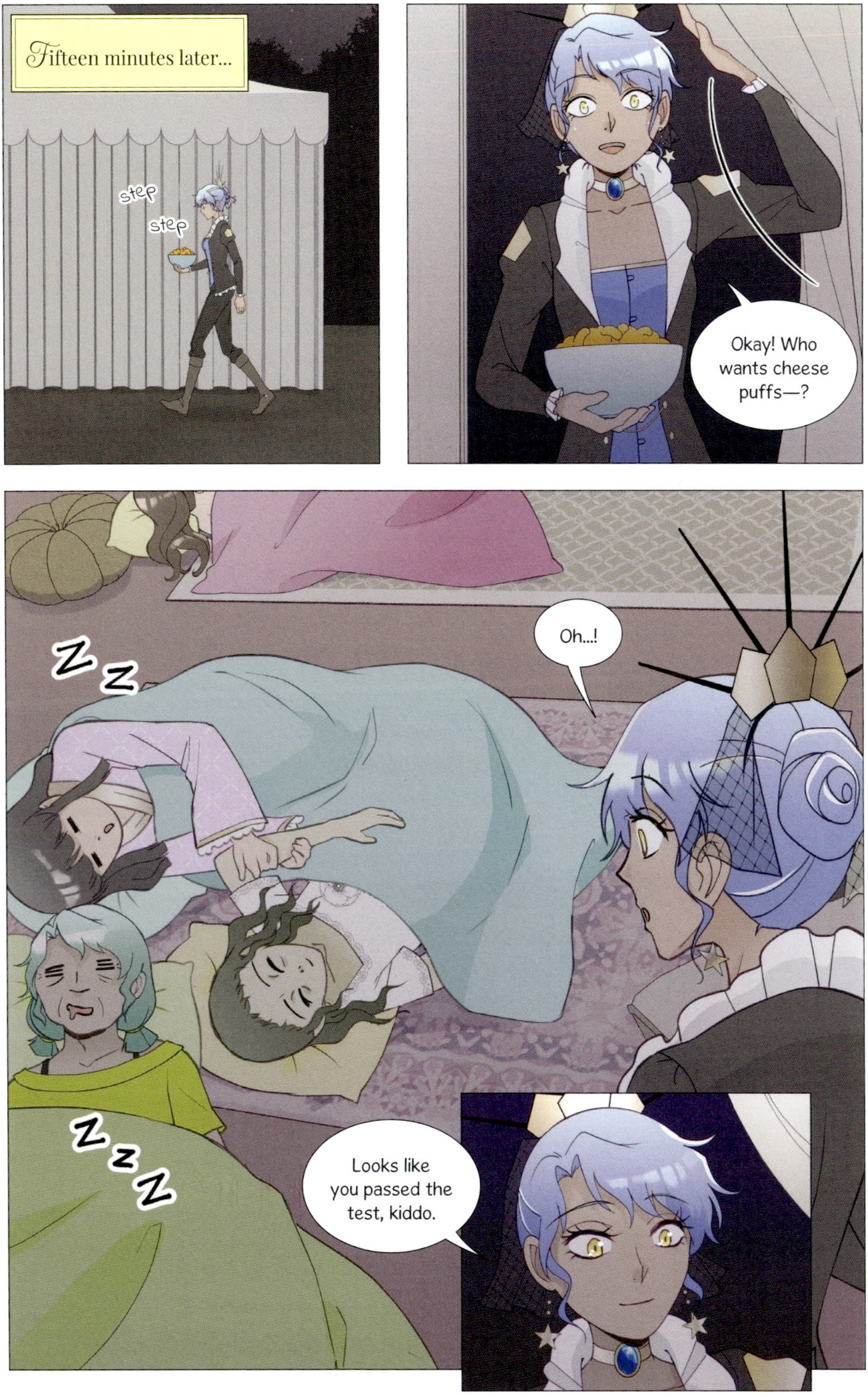

Oh...!

ZZ

ZzZ

Looks like you passed the test, kiddo.

Chapter 7

The morning after the slumber party...

Here's to Gwen, an official member of the Cursed Princess Club!

clink

Mm, I'm starving!!
Where did he come from??

Ah Gwen, this is my butler, Curtis. He takes care of the cooking and errands for our house.
It's a pleasure to meet you, Miss Gwen.

snicker
snort
Pfff
Hey, Curtis, nice buns...
These rolls don't look bad, either!!

I don't know what you ladies have scheduled in your planner for today...
...but I hope you have something loftier in mind than utilizing your extreme privilege to objectify the person who cooks and cleans for you.

So, Gwen, how often do you think you can stop by our club?
Some of us are here every day, while other princesses only come by occasionally when they need support.

Uh, well, since my family and teacher think this is some sort of institute I'm studying at, I think I have to come a few afternoons every week.
An institute, eh...?
I **do** sometimes give lectures, and I think everyone here can attest that they're not only informative but also very engaging.

Right, ladies?

Please don't make me tell a lie.
I wanna keep this nose for my date tonight.

I **do** think we each have things we can teach you about being a sophisticated princess.

Like how to talk to uncivilized, jerky princes you happen to be engaged to.
That's right! Today's the day the Plaid Princes are visiting!

Oh!! Do you think you're ready to talk to Frederick?
Yes!! I remember all your excellent advice!

Um, I also just want to thank everyone.
I was feeling really lost about things lately, and you all comforted me and helped guide me in the right direction.

You're welcome! Helping each other is what we strive to do here, after all!

Oh, Jolie! Before I go, I want to return your nightgown.
Thank you for lending it to me several times now!

Thank you! Come to think of it, where is your green dress?
I know I washed it and hung it the other day.

Gulp!

CHOMP
CHOMP
CHOMP
Monika, no...
You didn't steal that too, did you?

dash
IT'S MINE NOW, AND YOU CAN'T HAVE IT BACK!!!

Gwen, did you know that crows love collecting shiny and pretty objects?
She steals all our nice things and hoards it in her mess of a room!!

They make me feel happy and safe! Like this dress!!!
Monika!! Give it back!!
NO!!!!

I-it's okay! She can keep it!!
I made that dress, and it'll be easy to sew another one!
Oh my, Gwendolyn! You sew? I'd love to learn sometime!!
Can you even thread a needle with those claws...?

After a delicious brunch, Gwen said good bye and started her trek back home.

step
step
I didn't think I would say this, but I'm really happy I joined the Cursed Princess Club.

I'll never be able to thank them enough for their advice on how to resolve things with Frederick.
But first things first! I have to go home and get changed quickly.
I wanna make sure I'm fully prepared for the princes' arrival, unlike last time.

Good morning!
Welcome home, Your Highness!
Not allowed to make eye contact with the king's daughters

Hey, did ya hear the news, mate?
What is it this time...?

You know how some fancy pants princes visited the palace last weekend?
Well they're coming again today, and I heard they're gonna **marry** the Pastel Princesses.
Take it back.
Huh...? Take what back...?
I have to put up with your stupid, mean, work-inappropriate jokes all the time.
And when I don't get them, you call me a loser or a Granny Panties!
But this one **ISN'T FUNNY!!**

B-but I only tell you jokes on Tuesdays, mate. This was more of a gossip day...

I said **TAKE IT BACK!!!**
Or else!!!
...!!

Wh-wh-what's going on, mate...?
Are you in love with one of the Pastel Princesses or something?

Outside the Plaid Palace...
Come on, boys. We gotta get moving or we'll be late for our visit to the Pastel Kingdom.

Right away, Father!

But where is Frederick? I haven't seen him all morning!

Oh. I gave him a several-hour head start to travel to the Pastel Kingdom with Laverne.

Wait, Dad was actually serious about that...?!

Meet some princesses, they said. It'll be fun, they said...
step
step
Are you comfortable up there, Laverne?
Bleeeeeat!! (Translation: This is horrible service. Why haven't I been served a cocktail yet?)
I think there's only a few more miles until the Pastel Palace. Thank goodness...
I'm caked in dirt and sweat, and I smell like llama. Yet I still have to entertain a princess once I arrive?!
Why **should** I?!
Oh, that's right...because my life **literally** depends on it.

I mean, I guess I didn't even really talk to Gwendolyn much the last time...

I suppose it couldn't hurt to get to know her a lit—

Hey, Sunflower...

shake
Aghhh, I just want this stupid trip to be over with!!!

plop
Laverne, I'm not carrying you anymore! It's your job to carry **me**!!!

So...take me to the palace! I **command** you!!

....
Um... **please**?

AAAAGH!!!
FLING

Girl bye~
Ow, ow, ow, ow...

THUNK
I don't think this trip can get any worse.

WHOA! I guess it almost could have been a **LOT** worse...!

That's Gwendolyn, right?
I'd recognize that abhorrent dress anywhere...
What is she doing on a cliff out here...?

Ooooh such pretty, shiny stones!! I can't wait to take you all back home with me!!

Um... Gwendolyn?
Hello? Gwen??

Hmm, I guess I should move closer.
Might as well get this courtship over with as fast as possible.
step
step

Hey...
pat

WAAAAH!!!

slip
WHOOOOA!

...

POOF!

D-d-did
I...

Did I
just...

...MURDER MY
FIANCÉ?!

sob
You can't be serious, mate...
You're in love with one of the Pastel Princesses?!
Wh-which one?
sigh~
Princess Maria...
Don't tell me you've looked at her face!
I'm pretty sure the king has made that punishable by death!
No!! I would never **dare** to do that!!!
I've only heard her singing from the balcony above one of my guard posts.
But I don't need to see her to know that I'm in love with her.
A voice like that can only belong to someone benevolent, graceful, and beautiful.

I had it in my ten-year plan to gradually rise up the ranks and eventually ask the king for her hand in marriage.
But I guess I'll just have to speak to him now and demand that he cancel Princess Maria's engagement!

Okay, hold up... You think the king would cancel his daughter's engagement to an incredibly rich, hot, and powerful prince...
and hand her over to a shabby **guard** that he personally underpays?

...
Well, you don't know they're hot.
Bruh...

clip
clop
Gasp
They're here! Pull yourself together, mate!

You boys better be on your best behavior, because I'll be watching you like a hawk all evening!

Yes, Father.

Good afternoon, gentlemen.

step
step
They're coming up the stairs now!!
grip
I'm so nervous...
...but I have to act normal and try to find a way to talk to Frederick!
SLAM!
JACK! Get over here, you old crusty noodle!!!

Ahem...
Boys, show these ladies a great time. I'll be back to check on you in a few.
So much for watching us like a hawk...

We're so happy you came to visit us again!!
step
step

Thank you for spending your precious evening with us.

Oh, where's Jamie? We were looking forward to introducing ourselves today.

He's wrapping up a food critique and will be joining us in a little while.

Um... where is Frederick?

Ah, yes. Don't worry Gwendolyn, he's just running a little late.
Yeah and you'll never guess **why** he's late!!!
HE'S TAKING A LLA—

Shhh!
OW!!
JAB

Taking a lah...??

Err...taking a...l-l-long pee!
Frederick's late because he's taking a long pee right now.

Mm-kay...

I'm shaking...! I need to get a grip before he arrives!

I-I'm gonna prepare some snacks for us. I'll be right back!
Oh, why thank you, Gwen!!
stand

dash
So what would you like to do tonight? We'll go anywhere you'd like!

Oh...Um, Father never lets us leave the kingdom, so I don't think we can go anywhere...

Well, you heard our dads: we were instructed to show you a **great** evening.
And they'll be playing chess for hours anyhow. So how about it, ladies?

Well...okay!! How about—?

CREAK...

Oh...! Hey, li'l bro!

pant
cough

step
step

Umm... Blaine...?

I- I really need to speak to you in private...

Um...sure. I'm kind of in the middle of something, so why don't I meet you in the hall in a few minutes?

In the meantime, why don't you freshen yourself up first? You look...and **smell**... awful.

...Oh... Okay...

Please, please, please...
This can't be happening...
pace

wring
It wasn't on purpose...
I didn't mean to make her fall off that cliff...!!

I tried to peer down, but I couldn't find her body...
so I ran here to ask Blaine for help...

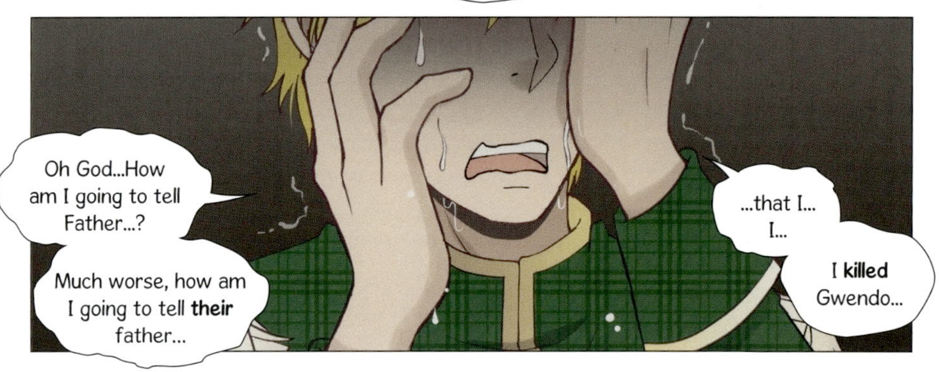
Oh God...How am I going to tell Father...?
Much worse, how am I going to tell **their** father...
...that I... I...
I **killed** Gwendo...

step
step
...lyn...

Wh-wh-what...?! H-how is she alive...?!
Was it not her that fell off of that cliff...??

gasp!
F-Frederick!!!
I'm not prepared to face him yet...!!!
I'm so bad at confrontation...! But I have to do this so our families can move forward!
sniffle
And no crying, no matter what! I need to be strong to do this right!!!
step
step
Ah, she's coming this way! Act casual...!

Hey, Frederick...
I know what you did to me...
Straining to fight back tears
Oh God, It **was** her that I pushed off the cliff!!!!
H-how did she survive that fall?!

Okay, I think that was about right. What was next?
I-I'm sorry!! I'm sorry...!!

It hurt my feelings, but I understand.
Got it.

It hurt. But I want you to know that I'm okay.
IS SHE TELLING ME SHE'S **IMMORTAL**?!

Ahh, this is so difficult! Just one more line!!

I'm fine not being your fiancé. I'll be watching you from the sidelines as your friend and sister-in-law from here on.
I just want you and everyone in our families to be happy.
Wow that's a mouthful.
Just keep it short and get it over with...!!
inhale~

LET'S BE FRIENDS, FREDERICK.
FROM NOW ON, I'LL BE WATCHING YOU FROM THE SHADOWS.
I HOPE YOU'RE HAPPY...

She's going to haunt me forever...!!!
I did it!! I communicated it all properly!
And he's stunned from my response, just like Syrah said!!

Now just muster up a big smile and walk away gracefully.

grin~
...?!

EEEEEEEEE—!!

slide
SHE...
IS DEFINITELY...
A WITCH!!!

I'M NOT MARRYING A WITCH!!!

CREAK
Okay, Frederick. I'm here. What's up?

Gw-gw-Gwendolyn... She's...she's alive... and I...earlier...
grab

Yeah...
I can't understand you when you're hyperventilating like that.
Can we be done here? The girls want us to take them to the amusement park in town.

Let's go.
tug
No—Blaine, wait...!
But, boy, do you still smell like Laverne.
Like a sweater soaked in a margarita...

Okay, we're all here. Let's go to the fair!

Yaaay!!

Can I come too??
Jamie!! You're back from work!
Yes, please come!!

Prince Jamie! It is an honor to finally meet you.
It's nice to meet you guys too!!

Bro, that wake of yours was **amazing.**
Could I get added to a mailing list for them or something?
Hahaha, I like you guys. You're funny!

SQUEAL~!

How did you get in here...?

Enchanté~!!

Chapter 8

step
step
Whoooa! This is what amusement parks are like?!

I've always read about them in magazines and dreamed of getting to go to one!
Especially on a date!

You all have honestly never been to an amusement park?
No! So we're open to any suggestions you have for what we should do here!

Is that so...?

I'm so scared!!
HAUNTED HOUSE
Hold Me!
It's not a cliché if they don't know know about it!

step
step
Hey, Gwennie... We've both been really busy and haven't gotten to talk much in the last week.
But for a while now, I've been meaning to ask you...
Has everything been okay with you?
Oh. I totally forgot...
...I can't really hide anything from you, Jamie.
Especially not between you and me!
So...I guess you probably knew something was off once you ate the waffle I made for you, right?
Well, actually...

As you know, my taste buds allow me to precisely discern not only many ingredients but also many emotions within people's cooking.
Each emotion exudes its own flavor to me, and it's allowed me to have a unique career as a food critic for many kingdoms.
The problem is... there are only so many flavors in existence. And some flavors and emotions taste practically identical to my tongue, which can really confuse my palate.
I once wrote a terrible review of a chef from the Paisley Kingdom because I thought he had served me Bolognese that fell on the floor.

Jamie's Journal of Identical Tastes

Excitement for the weekend tastes just like

Fresh autumn

Schadenfreude tastes identical to
Fried potatoes

Devastation tastes a lot like
Carpet
And one of my few crucial blind spots is that emotional devastation tastes identical to carpet.

But actually, his beloved parakeet had just passed away.
It's the grease stain on my conscience that will never wash out...
So when you made me that waffle after my wake, all I thought I tasted was carpet.
But I should have known that you'd never serve me something that fell on the floor!!
haha

pat
Ummm...no, you were right, I—

But when you baked us cookies for game night...
THIRSTY THIRSTY PRINCESS
I took a bite and definitely tasted...
munch

But it's gonna be fine now! I just talked with him and told him that we don't need to move forward with our engagement.
So I don't have to feel awkward around him anymore.
And all that's left is to convince Maria and Lorena to get married without me!

Sigh
It's all going to be fine now...

Well that's not fine with me!! He hasn't even gotten to know you yet!
I wanna talk to him, Sis!!

What?! No, Jamie! Please... You don't have to do that!!

Okay okay, if you say so...

DISGUSTING BLOODY CLOWN MURDERHOUSE
All right! Here's our first stop!

M-Murder-house?! I don't wanna go in there!!

The magazines never mentioned anything like this!!

Oh, but it's a quintessential part of the amusement park experience.

Just take my hand, and I promise to keep you safe.

Blaine...!

These arms are ready for you anytime...

Why are you holding them out like that?

That house looks kind of similar to the Cursed Princess Club headquarters...

Well, Jamie, shall we—?

sparkle
You and I haven't talked yet. I think we should become closer, don't you?
Wha—? I-I never once thought that, nope!!!
nervous laugh

Hey, guys! Me and Frederick are gonna have some bonding time, so go on without us, okay?
We're what...?!

Okay! Have fun!!
W-wait...!!
dash

The Perfect Relation-Ship

The Perfect Relation-Ship
Did you just see that smoking hot chick with the pink hair run in there with that dork in the plaid?
step
step
Ugh. Some guys have all the luck.

DISGUSTING BLOODY
CLOWN MURDERHOUSE

Welcome. Please enjoy each of the ten disgustingly bloody rooms we've prepared.
Uhh... thank you.

Blaine, I don't know about this...

Don't worry, Maria. Just stay close to me if you get scared.
...Oh, um... Okay, I will!

smile~
Haunted houses are such a blessing to gentlemen suitors. Why?

Because of their surefire ability to make a girl putty in one's hands.
It's a romantic and timeless recipe as simple as one, two, three.
tip
toe

01.
AAAAHHH!!!!
First, allow the nice clown to terrify your date.
02.
Then, as she turns around in fear, stand behind her with open and inviting arms.
03.
Watch as she melts in your strong embrace and falls deeper in love with you with each room.

rustle
By the end of the haunted house, these girls will be weak in the knees.
And so it begins...

BURST!
GIVE ME YOUR BLOOOOD!!!!

AAAAAAAHH!
AAAHHH!
VAMPIRE
CLOWN!!!

01.
Now embrace
me, my sweet
princess!!

BLAAARGH!!!
Ohhhh
no...
Fear vomiter

02.
KICK
AAAGH!!
OOF—

pant
pant
What
the...?

03.
I hate
my job.

Oh my gosh! Do you need help, Mister??

Scram, kid.

I just wanna be left alone so no one can see me like this.

OH, OKAY. I CAN MAKE SURE NO ONE FINDS YOUR BODY FOR A LONG TIME.

CHOKE

Is this what we do to people?!

Oh no, he passed out!

I'll find some medics once we leave the haunted house!

The Perfect Relation-Ship
Why did we go on **this** ride, of all things?!
I just headed for the nearest building!
But this is perfect for getting to chat with my future brother-in-law!
...
Um, I know that you and Gwen talked, and things are at a bit of a dead end right now.
Dead end? If anything, we're at an ***undead*** *end...*
No one should be forced to become close to anyone they don't want to.
But please just allow me to say...
Gwen is truly special to everyone who has come to know her.

I've tried dishes by chefs all over the world, and I've never yet tasted anything as lovely and **warm** as the food she makes.
There's something wonderful about her and everything she puts her heart into.

So...I'm just looking forward to the day you realize this too!

But anyway, the point of this ride is to get to know **you** better, Frederick!
Huh...?

Tell me what your hobbies are!
This will all serve as excellent future bonding material for Gwennie and him!

What? Oh...I-I don't really have time for any.

Oh, come on! Everyone has things they enjoy—or at least used to enjoy!
Agggh, too close! It's blinding...!!

F-fine.
Reading. I like reading books.
I mean I **used** to. And I built model ships when I was younger too.

Ooh, how refined!!!
Now we're getting somewhere!!!
Hmm, Frederick does seem more introverted and inexperienced than his older brothers...
Um, okay, Frederick. Just one more question...!

Thank goodness. I just want to sit in silence until this ride is finally over.

Have you ever been attracted to someone??
WHA—?

IT WAS AN HONEST MISTAKE!!!!!!
STAND
Mistake...?

Uh, Frederick! Please sit down, you're rocking the—
Ah...!

WHOA~!!

SPLASH

Chapter 9

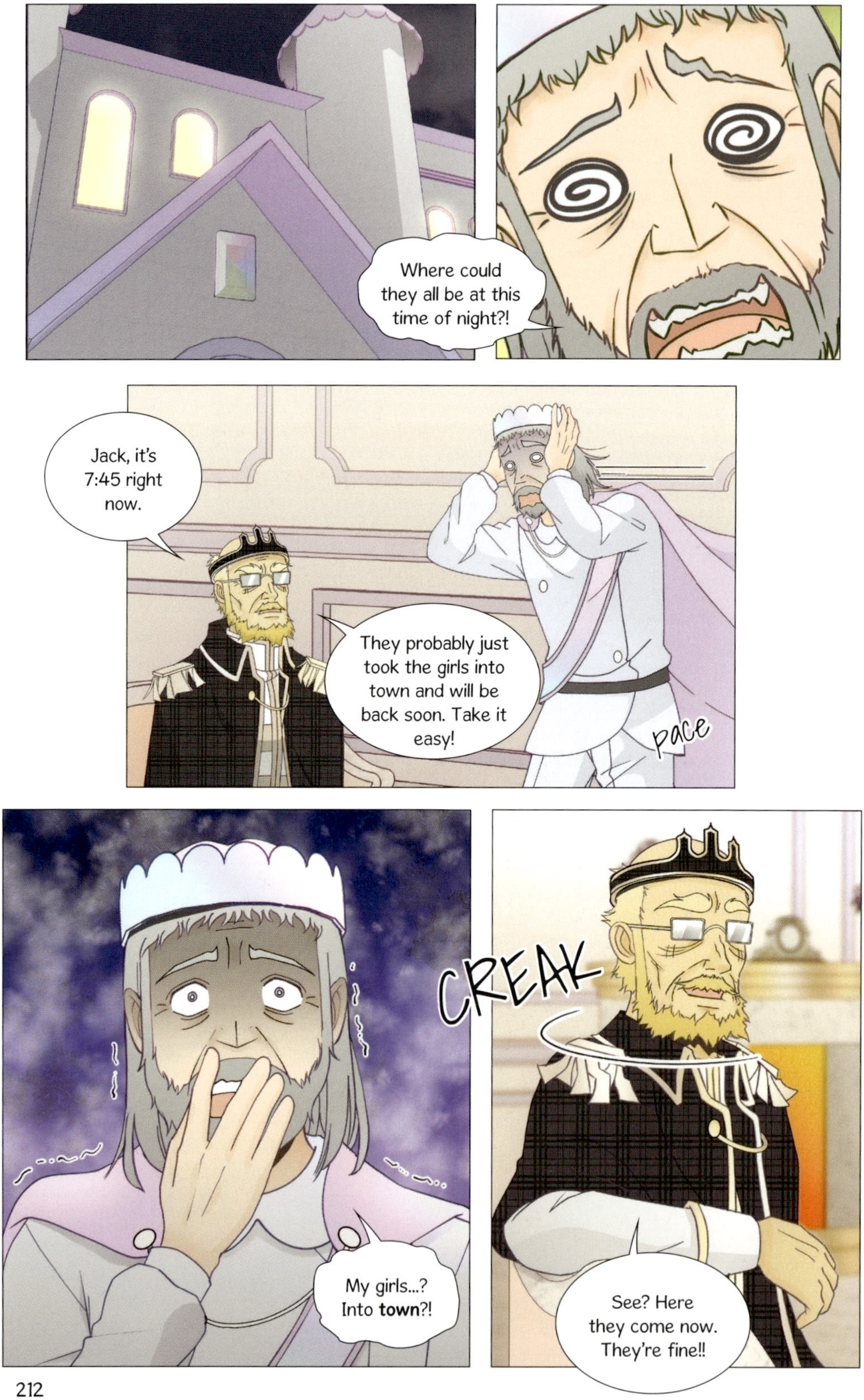

Where could they all be at this time of night?!

Jack, it's 7:45 right now.
They probably just took the girls into town and will be back soon. Take it easy!
pace

My girls...? Into **town**?!
CREAK
See? Here they come now. They're fine!!

We're home...!
Fake clown blood
drip
drip

WHAT IN THE DEVIL HAPPENED TO ALL OF YOU?!

Uhhh...

Hahahaha!
Snort

Haha... ha...

Achoo!

A short time later...
Oh, Father, we had so much fun at the amusement park!

Although I'm mortified that I vomited in front of you, Blaine.

Oh, please don't worry.
I can honestly say that somehow even your vomit is beautiful...
As well as quite patriotic...!
Oh, Blaine...! I'm ready to spend the rest of my life with you!

wring
M-my, you two already seem so... comfortable with each other...

Daddy, I KO'd like eight clowns!
It was pretty sexy...!
After it stopped being terrifying.

twitch
Yes, very nice, sweetie...
wring
wring

haha
chit
chat

Ugggh, somehow this trip to the Pastel Kingdom was even worse than the first one.
I had an exhausting journey with Laverne, then that horrific encounter with Gwendolyn.
And to top it all off, I fell into filthy amusement park water.
And of course, now I'm feeling sick too.

Um... here.

You were starting to look a little ill, so I thought I'd make you some soup...

You... made this...? For **me**?

Gulp

Such warmth...

Not just the temperature but the flavors, the texture, the feeling I have in my stomach...

How do I describe it? This soup tastes like...

kindness.

Is this what Jamie was telling me at the amusement park...?

How can this be from the same person who...who...

Amazing is an understatement.

I don't think I've tasted anything that good in... maybe ever.

I do feel better.
I feel comforted...
and relaxed,
and...

and...

Oh, I can take that bowl if you—

flop

So since we're all here and having a great time, let's discuss wedding plans, shall we?

Oh, I don't need to discuss anything— I could get married **tomorrow**!!!

Haha,
let's not joke around like that, sweetheart...

Well, I could have arrangements set up for a wedding at our palace as early as next week!!

Squeal
Really?! Yes, let's do it!!!!

Oh, Leland...! That's hilarious, but I don't think anyone **actually** wants to get married that quickly!!
haha

I want to!! I feel completely ready in my heart and soul to exchange vows with you, Blaine.
I feel the exact same way, Maria.

Well, Maria's always been the impractical one!
But, sweetie!! It takes a lot of time to pick out the perfect dress and flowers and decorations...

turn

Girls, **please**!!! I know there are a lot of emotions in the air!

But that's **exactly** why we need to remain calm right now and—

AAAAAHH

I'M POSTPONING THE WEDDING!!!!

pant pant
Father, what's gotten into you?!
Yeah! This whole thing was **your** idea in the first...

whimper~
...place...

...!!

blink blink
Erm...did I just nod off for a second?

...

W-w-wait,
was I....?!

Dang,
Gwen...

Hmm...
Attaboy,
Son...

I-I'm so sorry!!!
I didn't m-mean
to—
N-no, it's
okay...!!

I've got to hand it to you, Frederick.
I gave you an order to express your devotion to Gwendolyn, and you really came through.
It was maybe even a little **too** forward, to our detriment...But that's okay! I was moved nonetheless.
clop
clop
Huh?! No, that's not what happened—
Don't act so shy, li'l bro. Nuzzling all up on—

SMOOSH
Gagh, there's llama in my mouth—

Sorry, boys, Frederick won tonight...
so I decided we'd all take the carriage home together.

Anyhow, I'm proud of you, my boy.
Keep up the good work.

Sigh
The big day of confrontation is finally over, and I don't think it could have gone any better!

I already feel like a giant weight has been lifted from my chest, and I can almost relax again.
All that's left is to talk to my family tomorrow.
I'll tell them that Frederick and I support the union of our families, but we'd be happier as just friends.

Frederick...

W-wow, I think I'm really exhausted!! I'm just gonna get ready for bed quickly...

Chapter
10

chirp
chirp
blink
Z
Z
It's another beautiful day!
I feel refreshed and ready to talk to my family today...
about how Frederick and I don't want to get married!
Hmm, I feel like I'm relieved that it's morning.
Did I have a bad dream last night or something?
step
step
I don't remember...

GASP!
Oh. Right.

I-I've never seen anything like this...
Is this mirror broken or something?

FATHER, YOU CAN'T BE SERIOUS!!!

A List of Fatherly Decrees

In effect forthwith for each daughter until marriage.

It's simply a short list of some new house rules!
I just realized that I've been a bit too lenient with you girls!
Erm...Well, I don't really know because you've never let us talk to any other girls, but...
I'm pretty sure that's not true...
Anyway, I can't accept these rules!!
"While Papa is gone, no daughters are allowed to see the Plaid Princes nor let them inside of this palace"?!
Why, Father?! Didn't you want us to marry them so they would keep us company while you're gone so often?
Those have always been the rules here.
You've never been allowed outside the palace, and no one has ever been allowed to set foot in here while I'm gone.
And until you are married, there will be no exemptions to these rules. Not even for the princes.
But then why did you also push back the wedding indefinitely?!
B-b-because...! You girls just aren't ready yet!!!
Okay, but that's not even the most upsetting decree. Listen to this:
"During any interaction with the opposite sex, daughters shall only wear specific, father-approved attire."
What exactly is "father-approved" attire...?
Sigh
I expected pushback from this decree, so I came prepared with a sample.
Jamie, you can come on out now!

...BREATHE!!!

RIIIP~!

Well that backfired. Forget that rule, girls.

Then can we get rid of this next ridiculous rule too?
"No physical contact is ever allowed with the opposite sex, excluding family." None, like, at all?!
A nice compliment or curtsy can be just as affectionate as a love language.
A curtsy...?
So let's just cut to the chase and have you girls promise to abide by these rules, shall we?
And let's start with you, Gwennie-Pie!
No physical contact or letting any princes put their face really close to yours. Promise Papa, okay?
Gwen, you don't have to agree to this!!
Um, well actually, this is the perfect time to talk to all of you about something really important to me.
I think I can do this...!!
Oh!
Of course, sweetie. What is it?
Um...I've been afraid to say this because the last thing I want is to ruin Maria and Lorena's engagements...
or to hurt our alliance with the Plaid Kingdom at all.
But Frederick and I talked yesterday, and...
w-we'd like to cancel our engagement, as we both feel like there's no attraction between us!!

• • •
Uhhhh...
No... attraction?
Gwen is the youngest out of all of us...
and these new emotions have probably all been really confusing for her.
I guess we **have** been pretty selfishly charging ahead, which made her feel unready...
Gwen, you never have to worry about doing anything for our sake.
Nothing you do will affect our decision to marry or not so long as we know you're happy.
That's right, sweetie.
But maybe don't rush calling off your engagement. Why don't we just slowly see how things go?
Yeah, there's plenty of time!
Um, okay... That sounds fair.
I'm just so relieved they said they're not going to call off their marriages!!!

And fine, Father. We'll agree to slow things down with our engagements.
And we'll abstain from seeing the princes until after you've returned.
But we're not gonna do any of that other weird stuff you listed.
Well... thank you, girls. I appreciate it.
But I must have you abide by the last rule before I leave.
Another rule?! But Father!!
Girls, please.
Sigh
What is it now...?
The final rule: "Always remember that Papa loves you."
Oh, Father, we love you too!!!
Have a safe trip, Papa!!

FEE-FI-FO-FUNCTIONAL ALGEBRA

Oh.

Girls, if you miss the princes that much, might I suggest writing them a letter?
Throughout history, letter exchanges have been a creative and renowned practice for lovers to express their feelings for one another.
Not that I've ever received any...
Miss Agatha, you're a genius!!! Let's get started right away!!
We can also send them little gifts to remember us by!
Very good, Lorena! I like your proactive attitude!
And we've got paper right here!
RIP
That was your math textbook. Very bad, Lorena.
FEE-FI-FO-FUNCTIONAL
step
step
Hi, Gwen! We're about to write letters to the Plaid Princes. Would you like to join us?
Oh! Write a letter to Frederick? I'm not sure what I would even say to him, though!
I also have to leave for my extracurricular study soon...
Gasp
I can help with that part! I got to learn about Frederick on the amusement park ride!
If you can stick around for a second, I'll tell you all about it!
Yes! It's time for my romantic espionage to pay off!

A letter to Frederick, huh?
I do want to get to know him better now that we can simply be friends...!
So he likes books and model ships?
Those sound like nice hobbies!
Though it's a little surprising...!
Gwen!!! Welcome back! How did things go with Prince Frederick??
Oh, everything went perfectly, all thanks to your help!!
Yes, girl!! We wanna hear all about it!!

Hi, Prez!
Hey, great to see you, Gwen! Today's a fun day. We're gonna—

Make potions to reverse our curses!!!
What?! Abbi, no. We're not doing that.

Sigh~
Please, Prez!! I really, really need to try this **today**, just this once!!
Is today a special day?

Tonight's my school prom. It's basically the most important night in every teenager's life.
And when I think about walking out onto that dance floor in this stupid cursed body...I refuse to go.

But then I found this recipe for a 24-hour CURSE REVERSAL POTION!!!
If we make it now, I could have the magical prom night I've always dreamed of!!
DIY!

Abbi, you know that's not going to work, right? It's just preying on people's insecurities to sell magazines!
Besides, it completely goes against the pathos of the Cursed Princess Club, which is to love ourselves in our **current** form.

Yeaaah, but...
what if we all got 24 hours to be our old selves again?
Wouldn't that be **amazing**, guys?!
MURMUR
CHATTER

Oh my! I could go on a date with my Benedict again!!!
I could lie all I want without consequence!!!
Mm no, there would still be consequences for your lies...

But I could finally order at a fast-food restaurant without turning into a bird!
Ordering fast food makes you that anxious??
They ask so many questions, and everyone in line is waiting on me and... and...

B-but, guys... What would Princess Panda say...?
I wonder if this could be a good opportunity to learn what Prez's curse is...

Um... Prez?
Oh! Yes, kiddo?
Gwen still listens to me...
What would you do if **you** had your curse removed for 24 hours?

Nothing.
I can't take back the things I've done.
I can only take my past experiences and try to do something with them that can help others in the present.

PLEEEASE, Prez!! Just let me try this today!!
I'll never ask for anything ever again!!!
All I want is for Bobby to tell me that I'm beautiful and take my hand to dance...
squeeze
Just once...

Sigh
...Fine. But I'm not taking any part in it, okay?
pat
pat
Really?
THANK YOU, PREZ!!!!
Come on, Gwen, we gotta go to the market!!
dash
Huh?
I've got such a soft spot for little old ladies...

Welcome to the
Pastel Plaza
Thanks for coming with me, Gwen!
You like to cook and stuff, so I figured you'd be perfect for helping me pick out potion ingredients.
Well, I've never cooked with chimera blood or centaur hair before...
But I'm happy to help!
Okay, the last ingredient is brandy.
Who's Brandy? And what part of her do we cut off and stick in the potion?
What?! That's alcohol! We can't buy that— we're minors!!
Pssh, look at who you're talking to!
No one would even believe me if I said I was fifteen!
Abbi, we still shouldn't...
Oh come on, Gwen!! It's not like I want to get drunk or anything!!
I'm just going to **use** the alcohol to get a boy from school to make out with me!!

GRUNT
N-no, um...
...I-it's okay. I'm younger than I look...

S-see?? So just wait here, and I'll be right back, okay?

Abbi, wait!
stroll
Hey, little boy, Grandma wants to get lit.

step
step
Well, I tried to stop her...
Maybe I'll just wait in this store so I don't look complicit...

SALE
on our
least popular items!
Ooh, model ships!
Maybe I can find something here to send along with my letter to Frederick!

Yeah! I got some gifts to send to Frederick...

as a token of our new friendship!

Books and a ship in a bottle... This is what Frederick likes?

nod

Pfft, what an old geezer.

Okay, what's the next step in the recipe?
Let's see... Boil one cup of centaur blood with three raccoon molars and simmer for five minutes.
Hey, Gwen, where did we put the newt eyeballs again?
VALUE PACK! RACCOON TEETH
Um, the vial should be in the bag sitting on the coffee table.
Ah, found it. Thanks!
POOF!
Okay! I think it's done!!!

Hey, everyone! Who wants to try a 24-hour curse-reversal potion??

Me!!
I do!!!
Uhh, my cursed hand isn't letting me raise my other arm...but me too, please...

Hey, Prez, don't you wanna get in on this??
No thanks. I'm gonna go chop some firewood. You guys have fun, though!
Hmm. Suit yourself.

So according to this magazine, everyone who wants to participate should take a piece of paper...
...and write down a specific wish or reason they want their curse reversed.

After that, each person must drink a full cup of potion and kiss their scrap of paper.
The potion will take effect in a few minutes, and last for exactly 24 hours.

And Gwen'll be watching over us in case anything goes awry.
Cuz-she's the best.
It's the least I can do after all you guys helped me with!
So, everyone, grab a glass and let's do this!!!

Woooo!!!
Yeaaah!!!!

I want to be able to walk outside without making obscene hand gestures to people on the street...
I want to try on mascara...

Sigh
There's always just been one thing I've wanted...
...one thing that I'd do anything for...
GROAN

I want to walk into my school auditorium in my uncursed, teenage body and a glittery dress...
...and have Bobby approach me and say...

Abbi, I think you're beautiful. Will you dance with me?
Yes, Bobby!!!

SMOOCH!
Um Abbi, you've been kissing that paper for like five minutes.
I think that's good enough...

ahem...
Now we just have to sit for a few minutes and wait for the potion to activate!!
I'm so excited!!!

15 minutes later...
Any second now...!

45 minutes later...
I-I think I feel something tingling...!!

60 minutes later...
Nope. It was just my butt. It fell asleep.

Hey, Gwen, I made you a paper necklace.
Wow, Monika!

Yeah, I wrote down that if I didn't turn into a crow from anxiety, my wish would be to one day open a jewelry store.
Here, take a look in the mirror!

Do you like it?
GASP!

Oh my God, no...

Oh... Okay...
No problem. I'll just...come up with a new dream...

My face looked shattered in that mirror too...
That means there's nothing wrong with the mirror in my bedroom.
Is there something wrong with **me**...?!

Um, Abbi, darling?
While that was quite a delicious hair and teeth tea...
...wasn't the purpose to make our curses vanish?
If so, then why am I still in this repulsive, voluptuous human flesh?
And why has Monika turned into a bird again?
Yeah... Sorry I wasted everyone's time.
I guess this means I'm not going to my prom after all...

You sure you don't want to go at all? Even just to see your classmates?
No...I'll just kill the mood looking like this...
I think I'm just gonna go up to bed now...

Um actually, before you go upstairs, Prez said she'd like to speak to you outside.
tap

Great... I get to have her lecture me about why I shouldn't have been tricked by a stupid magazine.
Isn't being stuck in this body punishment enough?

step
step
Abbi...

Listen, Prez. I get it. I—

I'm no Bobby, but...
I think you're beautiful just the way you are, Abbi.
Will you dance with me?
YES!!!!!

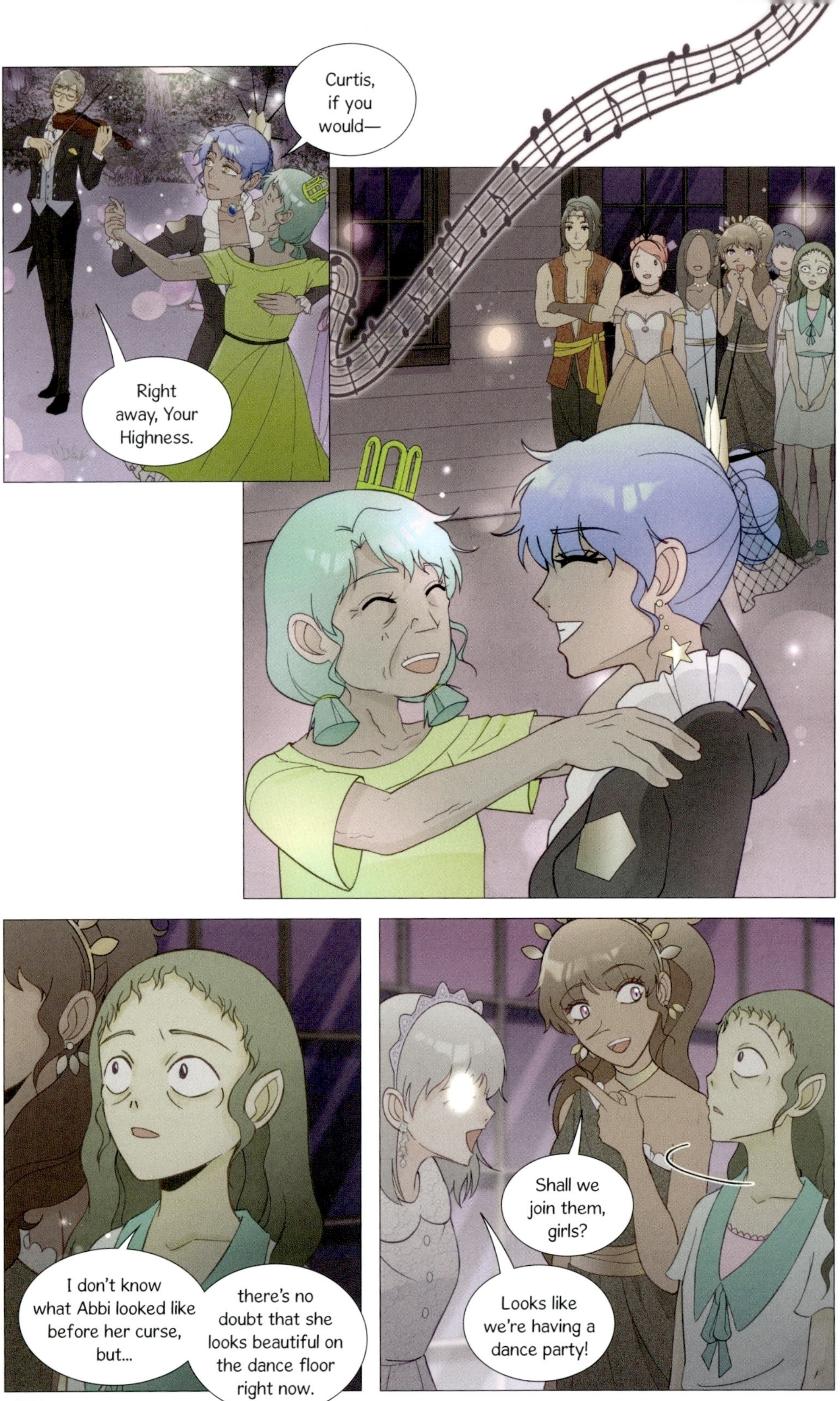

Curtis, if you would—

Right away, Your Highness.

Oh my, if that's the case, then I shall treat you all to a rare demonstration...
of one of the most sensuous and dangerous dances—the lobster courtship dance!
Do I have a volunteer for a partner?

Why thank you, Saffron!

What?! NO, you stupid hand!!
Is this revenge for drinking a curse-reversal potion?!

Let's go, partner!
But I didn't mean to volunteer—!!
Wait for me!

Chapter 11

You know what?! There's still a lot you could stand to learn from your brothers.

So today you'll be shadowing both of them during their daily duties.

And I can only pray that a **sliver** of their excellence will seep into that malnourished little body of yours.

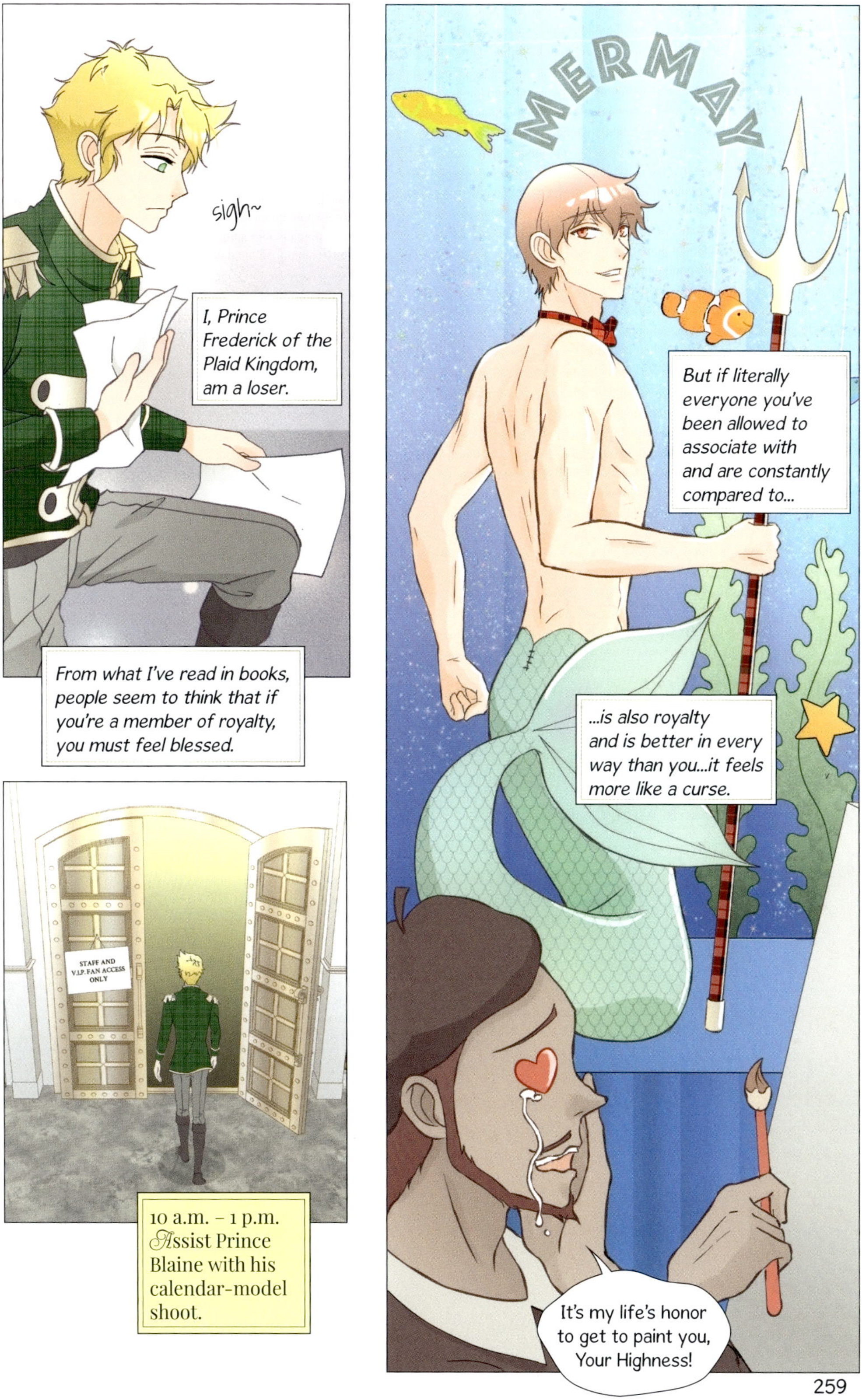

MERMAY

But if literally everyone you've been allowed to associate with and are constantly compared to...

...is also royalty and is better in every way than you...it feels more like a curse.

It's my life's honor to get to paint you, Your Highness!

Please marry us!!!
THE OFFICIAL PRINCE BLAINE FAN CLUB
You're pure perfection, Prince Blaine!!

Um, on the other hand... You over there, helping with the props?
I didn't even know this was possible, but your portrayal of seaweed is even more lifeless than the real thing.

So, Blaine... **This** is your important royal duty today?

Oh, I'm sorry. Does your personal brand bring in two percent of the national GDP and raise awareness for numerous charitable foundations? Hmm?

...No...

I'm well aware that I'm not perfect like Blaine.
1:30 p.m. – 3:30 p.m.
Assist Prince Lance in his sparring session.

And I'm not as strong as Lance.
It's cool you're helping me out, li'l bro. But you look like you're dying right now.
How were you able to survive your military academy training?

I'm fine!! I don't need you to go easy on me!!
pant
And I specialized in administrative support...!!

Oh, I see. Well, then...
WHOOSH!
...thanks for supporting me as I administrate this KICK!
AGGGGH!!!

Oh my God! I'm sorry, Frederick!! Are you all right??
CRASH!

I didn't always feel like a loser, though.
When did I start feeling this way?

Ah yes, it was my first day of military academy.

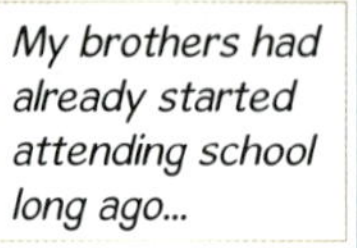
My brothers had already started attending school long ago...
...and were already racking up medals and accolades aplenty.

But I was homeschooled for many years due to a weak constitution.
I was alone for a lot of my childhood, but I didn't mind because I was enveloped in the vivid worlds of the books around me.

St. Cerulean's Inter-Kingdom Military Academy for Royal Boys
Welcome Frederick!
When I turned twelve, Father enrolled me midsemester at a separate boarding school.
I was so excited to introduce myself and talk about my favorite books with other people.

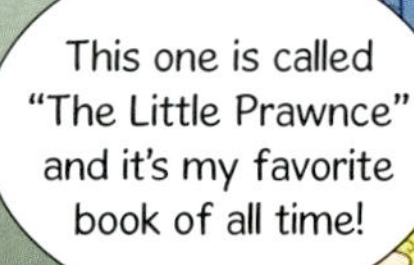
This one is called "The Little Prawnce" and it's my favorite book of all time!
Check out this dweeb, beaming like a frickin' sunflower over books and crap.
Makes me wanna slap that stupid smile off his face...

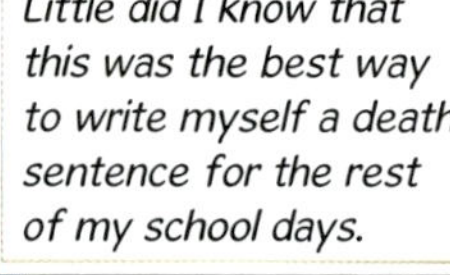
Little did I know that this was the best way to write myself a death sentence for the rest of my school days.

That was pretty fun for my first day of school!
step
step
And since I already set up my room, I can just read for the rest of the night!
WHOA!!
GRAB
Hey, Sunflower, we just wanted to give you a warm welcome to our school.
Nice room you have here... Think you got enough books?
Thanks! I was actually thinking I should have brought more—
SHOVE
haha ha
Shut up! I was making fun of you!!
Ugh, there's nothing worse than a dork who doesn't know he is one!
So hey, Sunflower, since you read so much, tell me...
do you know how long it takes for a sunflower to wilt in the dark?
Um, I don't really read botanical books, so—

SLAM
It takes just one night.

SMASH
RIIIP
LET ME OUT!! What are you guys doing out there?!
tear
crunch

They were right.

One night was all it took...

...for me to wilt.

By the end of my first day of military school, I had learned the harsh reality that I was a loser.

None of my peers would talk to me or even acknowledge my existence.

haha ha

I tried writing back home to Father for advice, but he made it pretty clear that I was not supposed to rely on him.

SINK OR SWIM, SON.

Is this blood...?

I dreamed of sailing far away from school on one of my model ships...

...or pretended I was the protagonist of every book I could borrow from the library.

But one day, an angel of fortune as beautiful and radiant as a thousand suns appeared above the man.
She had come to save him, and she lifted him out of the hole with ease.
With her by his side, the man became admired and respected by everyone.
With her faith in him, the man gained courage he never knew he had...
...and defeated a giant serpent that had been terrorizing the village.
The man was crowned a hero, and he lived happily ever after with the angel of fortune forever by his side.
I read this story over and over again to comfort myself that someone, someday would come and save me.
But as the years went by, I realized that I was an idiot to believe in such stupid fairy tales.

I graduated military academy with no honors or accolades, much to my father's exasperation.

Why should I work hard to impress people who never supported me?

If everyone was going to look down on me...

I decided I'd look down on everyone and everything first.

I was content living the rest of my life under that philosophy.

Until one fateful day...

All right, boys. Have a gander at your new potential fiancés from the Pastel Kingdom.
And don't say I never gave you anything.
When I looked at the portrait, I couldn't believe my eyes.
That's her!! That's the angel of fortune from the book, without a doubt!!
She was as radiant as a thousand suns and had a divine beauty that could make a man feel reborn.
"This is it!" I thought. I had lost hope, but she was truly coming to save me and lift me up.
With her by my side, I would become admired and respected by everyone and finally grow into the man I knew I could be.

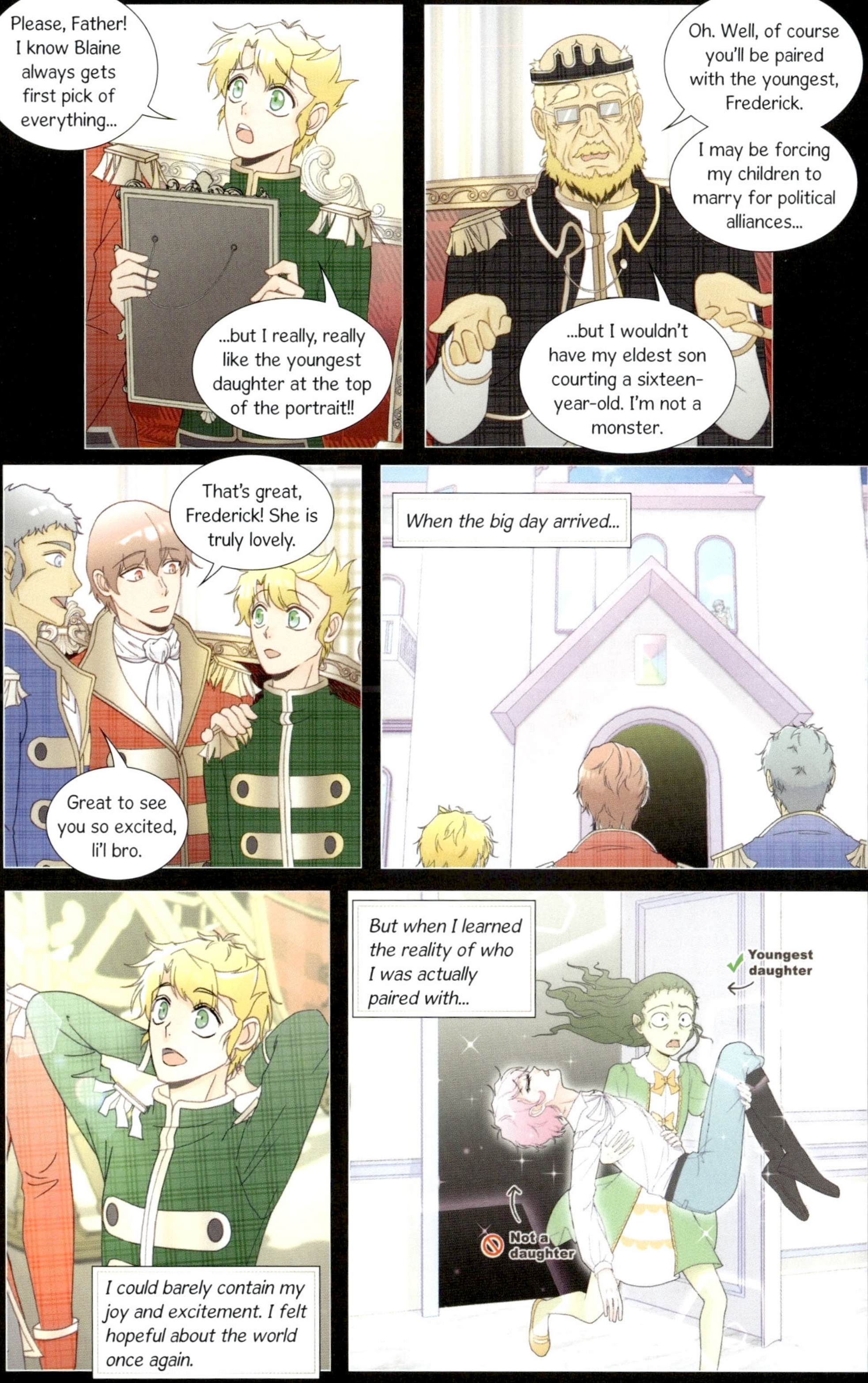

Please, Father! I know Blaine always gets first pick of everything...
...but I really, really like the youngest daughter at the top of the portrait!!
Oh. Well, of course you'll be paired with the youngest, Frederick.
I may be forcing my children to marry for political alliances...
...but I wouldn't have my eldest son courting a sixteen-year-old. I'm not a monster.
That's great, Frederick! She is truly lovely.
Great to see you so excited, li'l bro.
When the big day arrived...
I could barely contain my joy and excitement. I felt hopeful about the world once again.
But when I learned the reality of who I was actually paired with...
Youngest daughter
Not a daughter

...I realized I had vastly underestimated how cruel fate could be.
She did not come to save me.
At worst, she was a witch from a different type of fairy tale, and she had come to bring me a life of horror and despair.
Or at the very least, her physical appearance would not bring me admiration...
...but would instead drag me deeper into the hole as the village loser.
AAAAAHH!!
Oh, you're awake! Here, drink some fluids.
Huh?

Wait, what happened to me? Why are we in my room?
Well...you passed out when you were sparring with Lance.
And we felt bad for pushing you too hard when you were assisting us.

But also, we came to bring you this!!
Check it out, we each got packages in the mail from the Pastel Princesses!!

Yours was the heaviest, by the way.
Yeah, heavy like you and Gwen were about to get on that couch—
SHUT IT, LANCE!! I told you that's not what was happening!

All right, all right, sorry. We'll leave you to read your love letter in peace.
Take it easy, Frederick. Good work today.

...Thanks.

A package from Gwendolyn, huh?
As it turns out, Gwendolyn is much more confounding to me than I imagined.

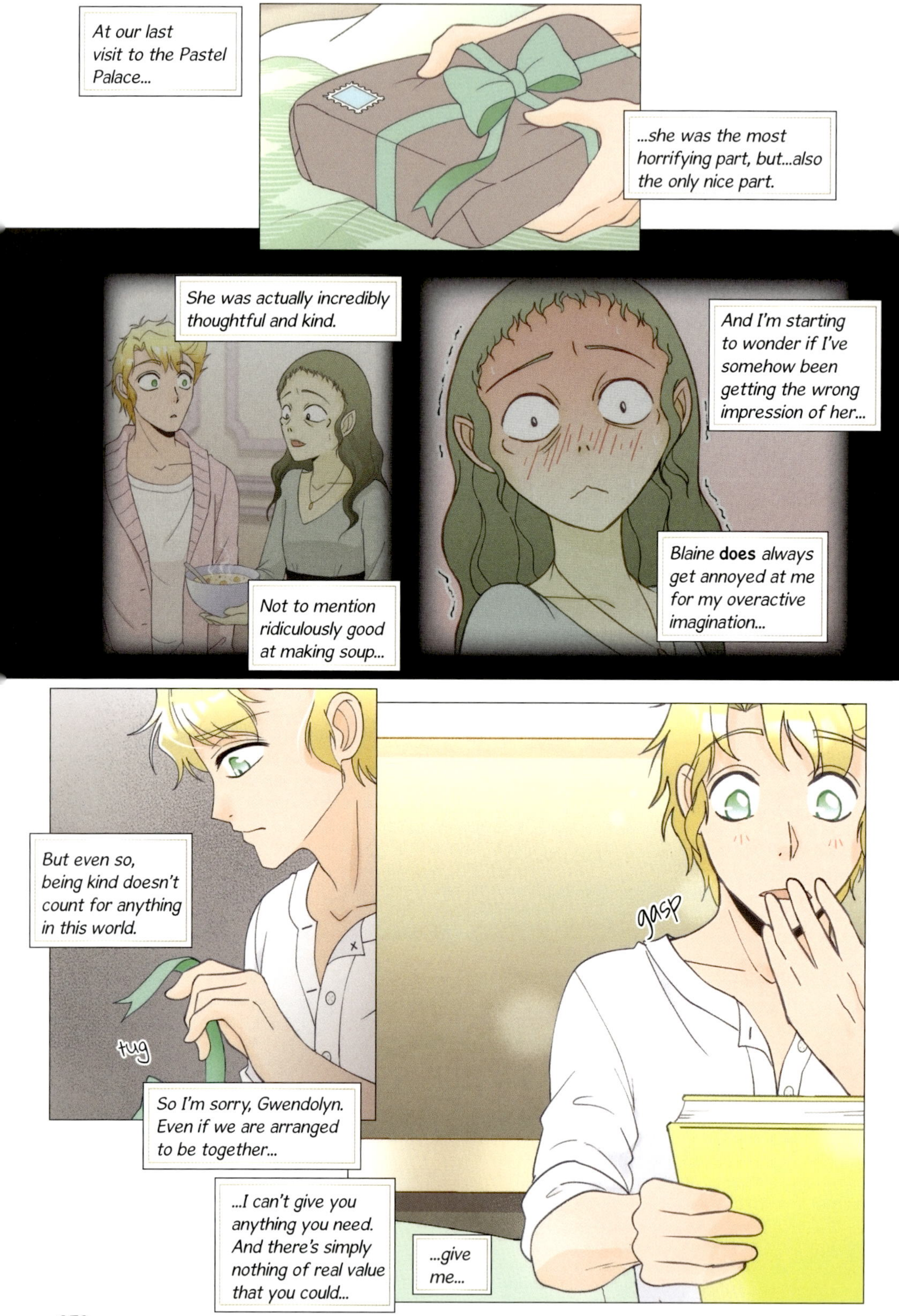

At our last visit to the Pastel Palace...

...she was the most horrifying part, but...also the only nice part.

But even so, being kind doesn't count for anything in this world.

tug

So I'm sorry, Gwendolyn. Even if we are arranged to be together...

...I can't give you anything you need. And there's simply nothing of real value that you could...

gasp

...give me...

The Little Prawnce
This is my favorite book from my childhood.
I never got another copy after mine got ripped up by my classmates.
There's a letter here too...

"Hi, Frederick. I heard you enjoy reading, so I thought I would send one of my favorite books.
"I'm afraid it may be too childish for your tastes, but it's a story that always makes me feel nice.
"What are your favorite books?"
My favorite books?
I've never told anyone after that day at school...

But...I mean, if she likes this one as much I do...
Maybe it couldn't hurt to tell her just a few other good ones...

"I also included a small charm at the bottom of the bag.
"I hope you like it! Warm regards, Gwen."
What is this feeling?

For some strange reason, despite everything I said, Gwendolyn can sometimes make me feel...
rustle

NEWT
EYEBALLS

...TERRIFIED!
That's right... Gwendolyn makes me feel **TERRIFIED!!**

At the CPC Headquarters...
gurgle~

BLECH!!

Wait...Where have I seen this little toy ship before...?

It was then that Abbi realized a crucial reason why their curse-reversal potion did not work.

To be continued in *Cursed Princess Club* volume 2

Early Concept Art & Character Design Sheets

Cursed Princess Club

Gwendolyn

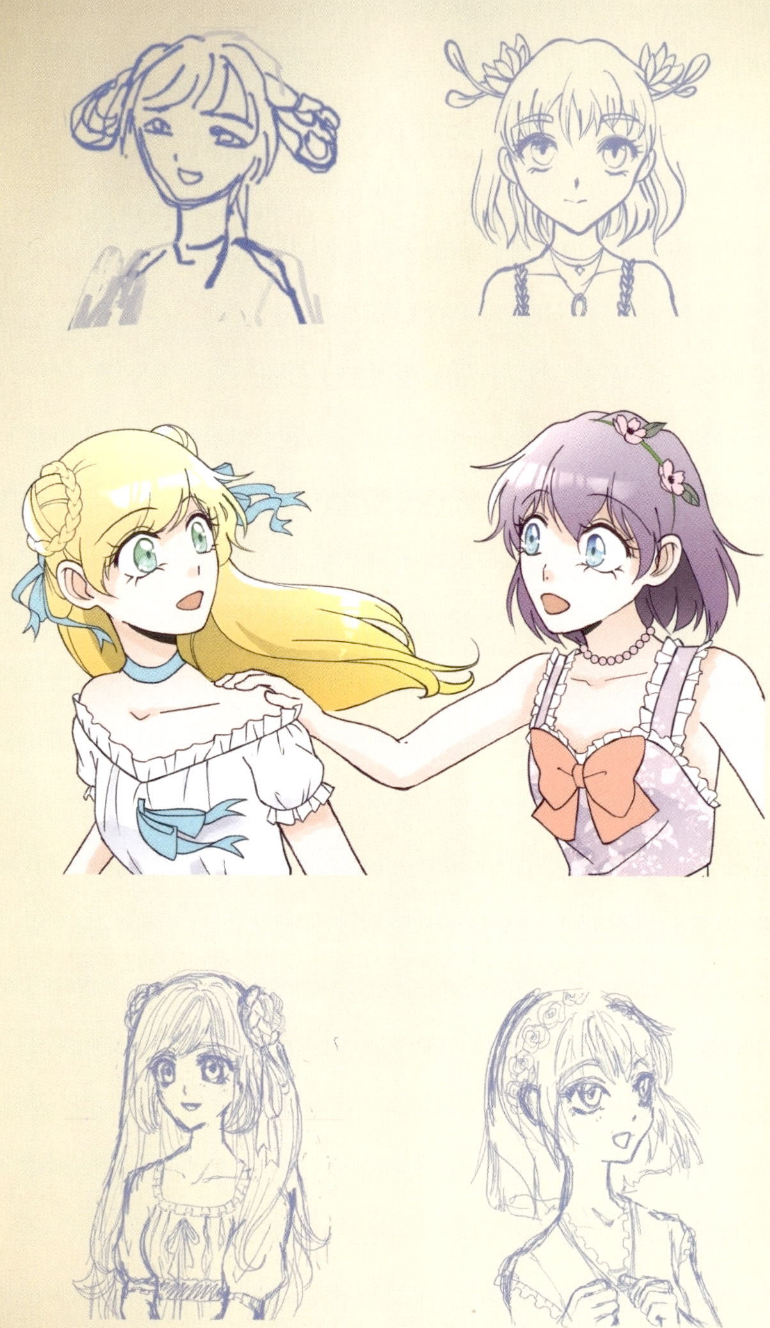

Maria & Lorena

The Pastel King

Frederick

Blaine

Prez

WHISPER
WHISPER
HEY, DID YOU SEE HER?
PEOPLE LOOK OVER THEIR SHOULDERS.

MURMUR MURMUR
GLANCE
GLANCE
I FEEL THEIR GAZES.

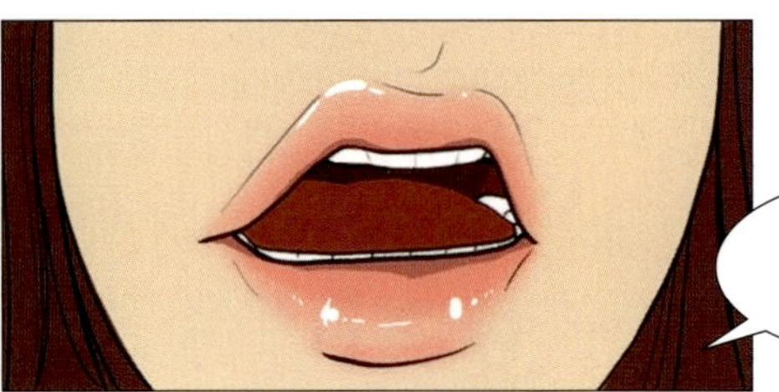
WOW, THAT GIRL IS SO PRETTY.

SHE HAS SUCH A PERFECT BODY.

2

LambCat is a small, omnivorous,
and easily frightened creature who has burrowed deep
into the Pacific Northwest to draw comics and make music.
They can be lured out by Bill Evans records and
frosted animal crackers.

Read the original on www.WEBTOONS.com

WHO AM I, YOU ASK?

A UNIVERSALLY RECOGNIZED

GODDESS!

YES?

CLICK

CLICK

I'M SO USED TO PEOPLE WHISPERING ABOUT ME.

CLICK

CLICK

CLICK

EXCUSE ME.